# Island out of Radar

# Island out of Radar

## LUCINDA FREEMAN

AuthorHouse™
1663 Liberty Drive
Bloomington, IN 47403
www.authorhouse.com
Phone: 1-800-839-8640

© 2013 by Lucinda Freeman. All rights reserved.

No part of this book may be reproduced, stored in a retrieval system, or transmitted by any means without the written permission of the author.

Published by AuthorHouse    03/15/2013

ISBN: 978-1-4817-3004-4 (sc)
ISBN: 978-1-4817-3002-0 (hc)
ISBN: 978-1-4817-3003-7 (e)

Library of Congress Control Number: 2013905006

Any people depicted in stock imagery provided by Thinkstock are models, and such images are being used for illustrative purposes only.
Certain stock imagery © Thinkstock.

This book is printed on acid-free paper.

Because of the dynamic nature of the Internet, any web addresses or links contained in this book may have changed since publication and may no longer be valid. The views expressed in this work are solely those of the author and do not necessarily reflect the views of the publisher, and the publisher hereby disclaims any responsibility for them.

# Contents

| | | |
|---|---|---|
| Chapter 1 | A Life Change | 1 |
| Chapter 2 | Bump In The Night | 4 |
| Chapter 3 | Horror on the Beach | 8 |
| Chapter 4 | Forty-Four Days and Counting | 11 |
| Chapter 5 | Surprises From the Sea | 14 |
| Chapter 6 | Redecorating My New Home | 16 |
| Chapter 7 | What a Feast | 18 |
| Chapter 8 | What is that Sparkle? | 22 |
| Chapter 9 | Becky, Need Help in Braiding | 29 |
| Chapter 10 | Lord, Let Them Be My Rescuers | 31 |
| Chapter 11 | Off Again | 36 |
| Chapter 12 | Meeting My New Doctor | 39 |
| Chapter 13 | How Did I Get Them? | 41 |
| Chapter 14 | The Call I Had Longed For | 44 |
| Chapter 15 | No, Not My Hair | 49 |
| Chapter 16 | The Return of Hair | 53 |
| Chapter 17 | Bonnie for Thanksgiving | 59 |
| Chapter 18 | My First Interview | 70 |
| Chapter 19 | Home For Christmas | 76 |
| Chapter 20 | My New Home For Now | 84 |
| Chapter 21 | Not Miss Margery Lord | 88 |
| Chapter 22 | "Let's Go Get Married" | 93 |
| Chapter 23 | What Is Happening? | 99 |
| Chapter 24 | Are We Going to the Island? | 104 |
| Chapter 25 | The Gathering | 107 |
| Chapter 26 | Home At Last | 111 |
| Chapter 27 | Reception and 4th of July Celebration | 119 |
| Chapter 28 | How Many Families Can We Find? | 125 |
| Chapter 29 | Miracle on Church Street | 128 |
| Chapter 30 | Where Did The Time Go? | 133 |

# Chapter 1

# A Life Change

The call was not what I was expecting for my mother was in good health when I left her.

Many times when Brad had received orders to move we always went to our home state to visit our family members. In the military you just go where ever they say. When Brad came home with the news of our transfer we were not pleased with the idea of going to Guam but it was either there or a remote tour for Brad alone. We had only been on the island for 7 months when I received that concerning call from my sister of my mother's stroke.

Brad was not too willing for me to leave him with the children but we could not afford for the whole family to travel. We can go space available can't we? I got the look and he said, 'And what if we get a lay over and we can not afford a motel?' I knew he was right but in the back of my mind I knew he did not want to take care of teen-agers, especially girls! Brad spent most of his career traveling from home so I was father and mother most of the girl's lives. I knew the Lord was in control of the situation and I felt now it is his turn to 'bond' with his girls.

The oldest son, Donny, was not too interested but assured me he would support the girls and they would be fine. I heard the assurance from our middle daughter, Becky, that she would help with the cooking and she and Bonnie, our youngest, would share responsibilities that had to be done.

As we hugged our goodbyes early the next morning I tried to joyfully tell them I would be home before they missed me. They tried to give me their reassured smiles and waved as I boarded the military transport plane for Hawaii.

I got comfy in my jump seat type chair and watched the crew members strapping cargo down getting ready for our departure. Several of the men came by and patted me on the shoulder and gave the few passengers a reassuring smile. Most of the passengers were military guys flying as crew or they had received orders for another base. Only one other family was flying as dependents so I was glad I was not by myself. As I was placed near an exit I was briefed by an airman who was by the door. He reassured me he would take care of me first if there were any problems. Now, that is all I needed to hear but knew it as important just as it is on a commercial airliner. I had to remind myself I am in the Lord's hands and would be fine.

As we were about two hours into the flight there was a big loud noise and the plane took a dive. The plane shook awful and I was praying that we were not going to crash into the ocean. Several of the crew members made their way to the cockpit and came back hanging on to objects trying to get the other family calm. I heard him say they ran into a flock of geese and the engines shut down and we were going to have to ditch into the water. As I heard the airman by the door remind me they had a raft and all we had to do was jump in. He tried to explain to us that he would go out on the wing and I would be handed to him and pushed into the raft. We were shown where our life preservers where and we were instructed to put them on and put our heads between our knees and hang on. We hit hard and I screamed with fright but didn't have time to lay there and feel sorry for myself. The airman jumped up, pulled the door open and climbed out in the wind and hung on to the frame of the door telling me to get up and take his hand. Sounded easy . . . . Only if you could move!!! I was scared and could not put weight on my legs so one of the other airmen came over and moved me to the door and the waiting arms of the airman on the wing. As the plane tossed about we had to move fast but it was so hard!!

I was so frightened but got through the door and stepped on the wing the airman pushed me off and I screamed out of my mind. I fell just as the wing came up and I looked up for others to be pushed into the raft but to my panic I saw the airman falling back into the door and the plane fell on its side into the black, cold water. I was screaming and watching the bubbles and waves pushing on the raft. For a moment I thought I was going to be thrown over board and the raft felt like it was getting sucked into the whirlpool of the plane as it sunk. I grabbed my shirt to see if my travel waist band wallet was still strapped to me and it was. It held my ID card, emergency family information and money for my trip. Whenever we traveled overseas I had to do that for I knew the children couldn't keep it on their bodies.

'Where is everybody?' I called out so they could follow my voice to come over to me and I kept calling and calling but didn't hear anyone as the sound the plane made the awful gushing and gurgling sounds and I knew it had carried my voice off into the sounds. As luggage surfaced I thought it was people and I would paddle over to it but found it wasn't a person. The waves were high and I put the suitcases into the raft to keep it buoyant for I was afraid I was going to be thrown out. I kept yelling as I prayed to the Lord until my voice was gone and then all I could do was cry. I felt so alone and questioned, 'why am I' the only way in this raft Lord? I kept watching what I thought was the area of which the plane went under hoping to see someone pop up at anytime. What seemed like hours, I didn't really know that I was drifting away from where I last saw the plane go under. I knew it was late morning so figured the planes would find me so I kept my eyes to the sky and horizons for the boats. 'What are they going to say to me when they find out I am the only survivor'? As I asked God all the questions in my heart I still could not understand, 'Why Me'?

As the late afternoon approached I thought, 'how can I survive the night'? They won't see me so I will have to lie in this raft . . . . ALL NIGHT!!! I was beginning to get cold as the sun was headed down. I opened a couple of the suitcases in hopes of finding some shirts or jackets to put on or wrap up in. The first one I opened was one of the airman's duffle bags and thankfully there was a uniform jacket. I searched in the backpacks I found water and snack crackers. Praising the Lord I heard Him say to sparingly find nourishment. In one of the suitcases I found a pocket flashlight and a pair of binoculars so thought these would come in very handy as I looked for a boat or plane overhead. I lie down in the center of all the bags and put them around the edges of the raft. The night seemed to make the waters calmer but I get car sick so wasn't handling the waves to well and praying to the Lord to help me not get sick for I needed the strength to watch for planes or boats. I knew the rescue teams would not find me in the dark but I was hoping that the raft would have something to signal for them to find me. I had seen this on television shows so had hopes this raft had such a device. I somehow got to sleep for my stomach was not feeling too good.

# Chapter 2

## Bump In The Night

When the sun started coming up so did the breeze. I was wet from the waves splashing on the raft and I had lain in the water all night so was shivering as the wind blew. I looked through the binoculars all around the horizon hoping to spot a boat but saw nothing. I was thirsty and had not drank any of the juice yet so felt I needed to sip a little. I also broke one of peanut butter sandwich cracker into and ate it. Which of course made me thirsty again? Next time I will eat the cracker and then drink.

The sun to my amazement was beginning to get warm so thought this is great to be able to dry out my clothes. In an hour I was very hot and knew I had to find something light weight to cover me from the sun. I opened the one duffle bag and found a shirt. It was large and as I tried putting it on it was like a sail and kept flying in the air. I lay down to button it at the top and let the breeze fill the shirt up and I used it like a sail. Wasn't thinking about where the raft and wind were taking me for I had lost all sense of direction so relied on the sun to know which way I was floating. All of a sudden I saw an airplane but it was so high up I didn't think it was a rescue plane. I quickly looked into one of the suitcases to see if I could find something that had a mirror on it but didn't find anything in two of the bags. By then the plane was gone in the opposite direction.

I thought I had better keep still and not use up any energy for I was not sure how long it would be before someone found me. The juice also didn't quench my thirst for it was too sweet but the sun was bearing down on me making me thirstier. I tried to sleep and keep covered up from the hot sun. I wanted to sing as I remember Paul and Silas did in the jail but found my voice couldn't handle it so just prayed. I drifted off to sleep several times and by now it was dusk and I dreaded the night for I couldn't see a thing. I could not see anything but water all around me during the day but it just gave me a little more security. I opened one of the briefcases to see if I could find a pen for writing. Thank goodness I found two tablets, pens and pencils so I took one of the pens and made marks on the front of the case as to how many days I had been drifting. Hopefully, if I was found I could tell them how long I had been in the water. I also wrote the date in case I didn't make it but they found the raft and would put it all together as to who I was with my waist band wallet. I didn't know whether to take it off or put it in one of the cases. I chose to wear it for now. As the sun fell I lay down and watched the beautiful stars and tried to remember all the constellations I had studied in school. It was calming and I must have fallen asleep.

Bump! Bump! Oh, no, what was that!!! I was thankful to be in the center of the raft and thankful that I had put the luggage around the outside so 'something' wouldn't reach over and pull me in the water. My thoughts of reading horror stories of sharks and whales in the ocean waiting to have a FREE meal came to thought. As I was praying for God's protection the bumping stopped and I was given the peace I needed and fell asleep. I woke up suddenly as rain was coming down and I hurriedly took the plastic bag I had crackers in and emptied them in the backpack. I used the flat brief case to let the rain run down it so I would have some fresh rainwater to drink. No sooner than I filled it the rain stopped. I unzipped one of the larger suitcases to find something to mop the water up from the bottom of the raft. It was mixed with the sea water so I knew I couldn't drink it.

As the night came to an end the sun was coming up and was very hot again sooner than I wanted it to be. I put the wet shirt on my head and scanned the horizon for boats and sky for help but saw nothing. I was thankful that the ocean was calm today so this made watching for boats much easier. Soon it was dusk and the darkness set in again. However, as I prayed for God's peace He soon gave it to me with sleep.

The best I can figure from my lines on the suitcase I now had survived 6 days with very little water and the snacks I had found were gone. I searched in all the baggage pieces that I had put in the raft and did find a gum package but nothing in the form of eatable substance. I was very weak and found I could not sit up holding the shirt as a sail any more. It did provide shade and when the breeze came up I used what strength I had and used it to help the raft move 'somewhere' faster. As the sun was falling I thought I had seen a dark area in the opposite horizon but couldn't fix my eyes to see it plainly. During the night I heard a lot of noise like surf and waves hitting against the side of the raft. Then all of a sudden the raft hit something and I thought maybe it was a school of whales and lay down in the bottom of the raft. I once again felt something under the raft and waited for I saw the sun was coming up and I would soon see what was causing all the noise and disturbance in the water. As I gazed around I saw large rocks and boulders in front of me and was so excited to think I found land and life. I maneuvered the raft away from the rocks for I was afraid they would be sharp and cut a hole in the raft. Thank goodness the raft came with metal paddles and I touched the bottom so knew I was in shallow waters. I climbed out and as I was too weak to pull the raft upon the beach so waited for each wave to come in and pulled until I finally got it where the waves would not take it back out. I sat down in the raft and looked for help thinking someone must have seen me but I waited a very long time and the sun was getting very hot for it was now high over me. I climbed out and found a group of palm trees and lay under them. I laid there for a while to cool off some and must have fallen asleep as the sun was farther down. I looked up at the trees and saw that they were coconut so started crawling to see if I could find one. Then I realized it had a hard shell and now I must find a way to break off the outer shell. Getting the much needed fluid that was in it was all I could think of. I crawled back to the raft and looked into a couple of the duffle bags hoping to find something to use. I had to spread it out on the sand and finally in one of the tote bags I found a hunting knife and began chipping away and finally found the little eyes to get a drink. Just as God had provided this I was able to drill into the eyes and drink what fluid there was. The groups of trees were next to a large boulder rock so I leaned against it and fell asleep. When I woke the tide had come up and it was under the raft so I quickly crawled back down to pull the raft up on the beach farther and picked up the items I had taken out of the bag and put it back inside. I went back to the coconuts and carried them to a large rock where I could cut off the outer shell and there I found another rock to try and break it open. After many tries and a smashed thumb it finally broke open and displayed the most tasty coconut morsels I had ever had. I knew I must eat them sparingly but thankful to the Lord for there were many on the ground that I would be satisfying my hunger. As the sun was beginning to fall, I knew I must find shelter for the night. I walked around the rock formations and saw a small low cave that looked like it had been under water before and had a carved opening. As I got closer and found it was wider than it looked from a distance so maybe the raft would fit inside. I crawled in hoping there were no animals or snakes but found I could scoop out some of the sand to make it deeper and be able to keep the luggage in the raft and have a place to sleep.

I thought I would put the sand scooping off until the next morning as I was very dizzy and knew I was getting dehydrated and needed something more to eat for energy to tackle that job. Plus I felt someone would be coming so I didn't want to use all my energy for nothing. With exhausting strength the Lord helped me pull the raft into the cave. As I crawled to find another coconut with water in it, I ate a few more pieces before going to sleep. The sound of the waves soothed my aching body and felt like I could sleep peaceably without being rocked to sleep. Crying to the Lord as I prayed for my rescue tomorrow I fell into a deep peaceful sleep.

# Chapter 3

# Horror on the Beach

After marking one of the hard shelled suitcases, before it got dark, I was amazed to see it had been 7 days since arriving on the island and 12 days that still no one had found me. I was beginning to feel stronger with the coconut juice and meat. I thought tomorrow would be the day I had to venture around the island for more food and water. Still wondering where the birds and crawly things were I kept looking in the trees and around the ground but hadn't seen anything yet.

I must have dozed off for I woke to the sound of water slapping against my new home and saw that water was entering the opening. All of a sudden I heard the sound of a motor and got really excited that I was going to be rescued. I tried to jump up and hit my head on the ceiling of the cave and it set me back down as I rubbed my head I could hear talking and laid down at the opening but I couldn't understand what they were saying. I didn't crawl out for I think the Lord had helped me by allowing me to hit my head to stop me from getting out and seeing who it was. As I laid there I could not see their faces but only saw their legs. All of a sudden I could see they were dragging a man down the beach. I quickly took sand and pushed it up around the entrance of the cave so they would not see the raft. They were walking away and dragging the man so I worked at hiding any existence of myself. Leaving a small hole I could look down the shore and watch but didn't like what I saw and I cried in horror for my safety.

When they had finished torturing the man they staked him to the beach and sat down as if waiting on him to die. One man stood up and looked my way and I just knew he was looking at my cave. He started walking toward me but kept looking back and out to sea so I moved more sand to fill the opening when he was looking away. I climbed back into the raft and cried hysterically shaking uncontrollable into one of the duffle bags.

God must have put me into a deep sleep and I didn't know how long I had been in the cave and was afraid to dig a hole out to see. I laid there remembering what I had observed and wondered if they had gone. I carefully pushed the sand away to gaze out but found it was dark so covered the hole up and went back into the raft to sleep until day light. Not knowing how late it was I kept making a hole and after several attempts and napping it was finally day break. As I peered out the hole I could not see anything up the shore to where the man had been staked. I made the hole larger and pushed my head out looking side to side as I inched out and finally all the way out I saw the boat had left. I went back into the cave and brought out the binoculars to look at the horizon and far out into the ocean I saw a large ship. I then looked up and down the beach to where the man should have been. The high tide had washed away any evidence that anything had taken place the night before. I gazed out into the waters and saw something floating and knew then it must have been the dead man. I kept the binoculars with me and climbed upon a high boulder and scanned the horizon watching the large ship disappear into the horizon and wondered if those men would be coming back again. As I climbed down I sat under the palm trees against the large rock and rested my head against it but I couldn't believe what I was hearing for I could hear water running. I crawled around the other side carefully listening by putting my ear against the rock. I found the boulder solid with no opening so went back around to where I heard the running water. I thought maybe that was why the trees were all there and it might have a spring under that side that feed them. I dug but found nothing. The sun was beginning to show itself at the horizon so I knew I must hurry to find food and water. I walked to the other side of the island and found more groves of trees which were all some kind of fruit. Crying and praising the Lord I knew it all had come from him. With this in mind, I started singing His praises for I knew he also would direct me to water. I gathered up the yellow skinned fruit of which I thought was a Papaya but so much larger than in grocery stores and mangos with pink on the skin. My mouth was watering as I carried them back to the raft. I found the mango was sweet and juicy so knew it provided some fluid for me until I could find the real thing! I was not feeling very well as my monthly cycle had come to visit me. I found some T-shirts so made due for the next 4 days. Much to my astonishment as I washed them in the ocean I saw a few fish swimming around and once saw a small shark.

It was relaxing to walk the beach each morning early before the sun came up but still light to see. I found a group of large rocks some sitting in the ocean and some on the shore line. I sat there for a little bit and thought what a gorgeous sight with the sun coming up. I sat there praying for the Lord to help me find water and most of all to guide someone to rescue me. I started walking down the other side of the island, keeping in mind that anything I found on the beach that had been washed up overnight might be useful. I carried drift wood along with a couple of large pieces of hard foam and thought somehow they might come in handy for something. Then I wondered where I could hide them if those bad guys come back. I sure didn't want them to wonder if someone was on the island and start looking around. I placed them amongst the trees hoping they would think they had floated up there during a storm.

As I rested after my walk I sat back under the trees and against the cliff and once again heard the water sound. Looking up the rock I wanted to climb on top and see if there was an opening somewhere on it. I decided to crawl at the lowest edge and work myself up. It was a wide boulder and plenty of grooves for putting my feet in for leverage. When I got to the top I could not see any openings but turned around and sat looking out along the horizon. I spotted something floating to the beach so crawled back down to go see what it was. As I got to the edge it had disappeared so thought it must have floated on out to sea.

Before it got too dark I didn't want to forget to mark the briefcase of the day the men had visited the island. I ate some more fruit listening to the waves. Finally I got out and covered the entrance with sand but leaving a small opening for fresh air and went to sleep.

## Chapter 4

# Forty-Four Days and Counting

In my mind I thought no one was coming now as I looked at the marks on my suitcase and counted that 44 days had gone by. I took my usual stroll along the beach looking for any objects that would help my stay until someone found me. I did gather drift wood and decided tonight I would build a fire and try to catch some fish. As I was looking for a good place that might be deep enough to have fish in it I saw an object in the water coming toward the island and ran to the small cave. I always ran on the wet sand because for some reason the Lord had put a fear in me to hide evidence that I was on the island. I heard the sound of a boat motor and sat there waiting and watching the opening of the cave entrance praying that it wasn't those bad men again. There was always a breeze and the sand was dry by the cave so my footprints had been swept away as the sand filled them in. I heard voices but again could not understand the language. Then I heard a gun shot and I started crying. I was so afraid they might have seen something to make them think someone was there. As soon as they came they left but of course I didn't know what the shot was so waited for a long time before crawling out. When I did I looked to where I heard the sound and saw a body laying in the water at the edge and it was drifting out into the ocean. My mind could not understand why this island seemed to be a burial ground for these men. What could they have done that was so horrible that they were killed in this manner?

I grabbed the binoculars and ran to the large boulder and climbed up on top to see if I could spot the motor boat but saw that same large ship in the distance so had a bad feeling that it must be a large group of bad men like pirates or drug smugglers. I did not know this but only what I saw on the news when something like this happened to other boats taken hostage by them. As I crawled to the center of the rock to look around at the whole horizon I turned and the rock crumbled beneath my knee and quickly crawled to the edge for I was afraid it would collapse under me. I laid my whole body flat and picked at the hole and all of a sudden I heard the sound of water. I crawled down off the boulder and ran to get a rock that would be the shape of an axe type so I could chip away at the top of it. I found the right size and climbed back on top to break the rock away. Once I had about a two by two foot hole made I looked down in the hole but it was pitch dark. I thought maybe when the sun rose overhead it would shine down in it and I could see if there was a spring. I took one of the broken rocks and tossed it down but couldn't hear it hit. I thought it must be very deep, but then it might be shallow and full of sand.

I remembered in one of the suitcases a small pocket flashlight. I was thinking at that time to use it if I saw a plane or boat. I ran to fetch it and of course the flashlight was not of high power but at least I could see it was a deep cave but had a floor of sand. As I hung my head I saw that it was as big as the boulder approximately 30 feet long and 20 wide but couldn't tell as the walls were black and too dark to see clearly. As I was trying to figure out how I would get down into the cave I remembered the raft had a rope tied to it that went all around it. I climbed down and untied the rope from the raft and carried it back to the top of the boulder. Looking at the closest three palm trees that were standing very close to the edge of the rock I wondered if I could throw it over one of the large leaves and pull it to me. I knew one slip and I would fall to the bottom of the cliff and break something so praying for help I made a large knot at the end and swung it into the farthest tree. It caught on a limb and I pulled it toward me. I did the same to the other two and tied the rope around all 3 for holding me as I climbed down. I remembered in Girl Scouts how to tie knots in ropes for climbing and praised the Lord for remembering how to do it. Noticing and feeling the sun overhead it was getting very hot. I knew I would have to hurry in order to see anything in the cave. I slowly climbed down into the large cave and as my head cleared the top I took the flashlight and put it in my mouth to move it toward the sound of the spring. As I gasped with excitement the flashlight fell out of my mouth to the bottom and fell on the sand. Much to my delight its light balanced off the rock and showed me the floor of the cave. My God is so AWESOME!!!! I was so weak with excitement and tired from the climb I crawled to the water and washed my face in it. It tasted so wonderful so I drank from my scooped hands and cried. I picked up the flashlight and turned it off to get accustomed to the darkness of the cave and focusing on the light shining through. As I sat there it became easier to focus on the walls of the cave and saw it had rock formations like a cavern sticking out from them. The spring was coming out of the tree side but flowing back down into the sand. The other side was solid and dropped toward the ocean. The spring had made a small pool and I thought if I am to stay here for a while I would put rocks around it to make it deeper to sit or lay in. As I took slow small drinks of water I started focusing better and not feeling as dizzy as I moved around. I had not even thought to shine the flashlight around to see if I was the only one there or had been there. Then thinking, I had to break through the top so how could there have been someone there before me. I leaned against the wall of the cave and felt the coolness of the sand and was trying to get my eyes adjusted to the darkness that I think I must have taken a nap for when I woke up the sun was not shining in the cave. I thought I had better hurry and get out so I could see. When the moon shines at night it is such a beautiful glow that you can walk the beach without worry. However, in the cave there is only darkness.

As I went back to my little cave I made plans as how to get all the bags down into the larger cave. I knew the raft would not fit but could make the bags fit. I was thankful for the smaller cave for if I was caught walking the beach and a boat came I could run to it and hide. I knew God would let me know when someone safe was coming.

The next day came I woke up and peeked out to see it was getting light so I ran down to my rock at the far end of the island. I had adopted it for my 'worship' rock and was praising and thanking the Lord for keeping me safe and finding me a better place to live for the time being. As I sat on my rock I looked all around to the horizon for any sign of boats. Getting down I made my trips around the island picking up drift wood and grass for my bed and to make a fire. Carrying them wasn't hard but thinking of putting it down into my new cave I had to throw the wood to the top of the boulder I climbed up and dropped the pieces down into the cave. I got more and more excited to know I could stand up in my new home and have plenty of room to walk around in it. I put the binoculars on top and scanned the horizon again. Not seeing anything I decided I would bring the bags. Crawling to the top with each bag in hand was pretty hard as they were heavy from the ocean water leaking in them. It took me all morning to get them up and dropping them down into the cave. Thank goodness the larger ones were not where duffle type bags so I could take out some of the clothes and then get them through the hole. Now I knew I could start a fire in my new cave and not worry about it blowing out and I could cook some fish. My energy would get better with some protein in my system.

# Chapter 5

## *Surprises From the Sea*

Now the sun was overhead and I could see in the cave better. I carried all my fruit and coconuts in one of the duffle bags and decided I was getting weak again so needed to eat something. Taking my palm branch and smoothing the sand all around from the little cave to the boulder covering my footprints and from where I had drug the luggage. I opened one of the small brief cases I found the tablets of paper, two pens and three pencils. I put them in the sun as they were damp and I needed them dry to write on. Marking the leather briefcase that kept the record of my days since the crash I now could keep them on paper and even doing a journal maybe. Needing to count the days between visits from the bad guys was important for me to keep track and be ready and watching.

All my 'treasures' were in the cave so I sat at the top taking my binoculars and looking around the beach for anything I missed or looking for that big ship to appear. Thinking the large ship is the first thing I needed to look for, as the little boat comes when the larger ship is near. Looking at the place where I thought the boat must have docked I saw a familiar box floating close to the beach. This time is was much closer and I thought it might drift in. I climbed down and walked to the beach and watched it get closer and closer. Finally I could wade out and pull it to shore. It was secured with duct tape all around it and now it was clear why it was easy to spot in the water. However, there was a hole and a piece of drift wood sticking in it. I pulled out the stick and ran up to get the knife to cut it open. It was very heavy and thought whatever was in it might not be any good for the ocean water would have gotten in it through the hole. Taking the knife I tried to cut the tape but it was really thick so wedged it against a large stone and jabbed hole in it along a straight line at the edge and then cut into it. Getting enough cut to pry open a corner I pulled out small plastic bundles about 3 x 6 x 4 and laid them down on the sand. I counted 50 bundles. I cut open one of the bundles thinking maybe it was dope and these had been drug smugglers so carefully tried not to cut into the bag. Finding the opening I folded it back and found bills of money!!! Oh my, I thought. This is what they have been coming to the island to get I'll bet. I ran back to my cave and brought one of the smaller duffle bags and put the money in it. Then I took the drift wood and some rocks and stuffed them into the package. As I ran to the other end of the beach to where the current flowed away I threw it into the water. It started floating out into the ocean. I ran back along the wet sand and realized I had not gotten the palm branch that I carry. So I carried the bag up to the edge of the cliff and ran back to cover my tracks. My heart was beating so hard I was scared they would be coming back that day for their 'stuff'. I climbed to the top and looked all around to see if I had left anything lying on the beach and realized I had put it all in the bag. Still shaking from my 'find' I couldn't get my heart and mind to quiet down and started thinking of what I was going to do with it. I prayed to the Lord that I hope it was not wired to explode or anything. "that is what I get for watching too many of those spy movies,' I said to myself. I drank some water and laid back on two of the duffle bags and looked at the small sturdy bag that held all that money.

Trying now to figure out how much 'treasure' I had lifted from the ocean and thankful that the money was not wet I started to count one of the packets. I gasped as I now thought this can't be real money but knew it was. In the first one I counted $5,000, and then the next and the next figuring there must be $250,000 in bills that I have in this bag! I was so exhausted from counting I got into the little pool and just soaked for I just couldn't imagine having that much money in my position. Now I am really worried for my safety but if I am captured I would be tortured, raped and killed I am sure. Every day is going to be spent watching for this danger. I trust you God for you have kept me safe so far and I know you are watching over me now.

I looked at the entrance hole of the cave and it was getting dark but couldn't remember resting and the afternoon had gone so fast. I climbed up and heard thunder off to the west and the wind was coming up. I didn't want to go back out and fish so ate some coconut meat and Papaya. Tomorrow would be the day for fishing and fixing up my new cave.

# Chapter 6

# Redecorating My New Home

I woke up this morning feeling excitement as to the many things I had planned to do. I still couldn't get the bundle of money that had drifted to my front door out of my mind. I decided before I ventured out I would bury the money in the bag in the far side of the cave that was higher in case the cave flooded. My eyes had adjusted to the cave light so was able to eat the other half of Papaya. I was so nervous last night to eat it all. I tried to climb to the top to see if the storm brought me any goodies. As I climbed I felt I was not able to pull myself up as fast and my arms really were hurting. I should drop some rocks down to help climb out maybe. On the side of the cave where I put the rope were a few rocks that jutted out and I used them to support my footing. I climbed out but knew I would have to lift lots of rock to make it easier. As the sun was not up, I peered around the horizon and beach before I climbed down. Finding no ships at the horizon I walked to my worship rock for praising and singing to my Lord. "I need for you Lord to help me with this money that I found! What am I to do with it for where would I spend it as long as I was here. It tells me Lord I am going home or you wouldn't have allowed me to find it".

Walking the beach later I kept a watch for the ship for I just couldn't help but think they would be back looking for the 'package'. I found a few pieces of drift wood and a couple of pretty shells that I took back to the boulder to take down later in the cave. Maybe I could take a couple of these back for keep-sakes to remember my stay here.

I felt I could now hang the clothes on the cavern type rocks coming out of the walls like a 'hanger'! Putting the drift wood in the sunlight I wanted them to dry so I could light a fire. The cave was very damp from the small water fall. I thought maybe a fire might dry it up some and the smoke would kill any mold over time. I am not a fish lover but the thought was making me hungry, and yet would not like to think about having to eat them raw. As only God could do I found three cigarette lighters in a couple of duffle bags. Hoping they were not ruined by the sea water I laid them on a rock where the sun could possibly dry them off. I hoped it wouldn't evaporate the lighter fluid. The sun opening could not cover all the things I needed to dry. I went back up to the top of cave and looked around cautiously but saw nothing so pulled the empty duffle bags up. I laid each of them in the sun to dry. They were to damp too lay on, but I knew when it was dry I could use it to start a fire.

By now the sun was directly overhead so I couldn't walk the beach until later in the afternoon. I went down and lay against the wall of the cave and fell asleep for a short time. When I woke up I crawled out carefully and looked around before crawling down off the cliff. I found the sun and hot rock had dried the bags. Thinking to myself that was not a smart thing I had just did to leave the bags up on top and fall asleep. What if the boat had come? Dropping them down I decided to walk part of the island and look for a good deep place to fish. Noticing in certain places when I walked I could go quite a ways out in the water for there were not large waves coming into shore. The only place was down by my worship rock so figured the water was deeper there. In fact the place where the boat had come was about the deepest I thought for the boat wouldn't have pulled up in the shallow reef area. Finding only a couple of beautiful Conch shells I knew they had good meat in them but not knowing how to get the meat out was something I would have to figure out. I could use that meat for bait so took one to the cave and put it upside down in the water that flowed from the spring that went somewhere underground near the grove of trees. This will be my project for tomorrow. Picking up more fruit would be my supper and the Papaya's were so very ripe and juicy.

I called it an early night for the sun was just taking all the strength out of me anymore and I felt like I was getting anemic from the loss of blood from my cycles. Dusk was now upon me so knew I needed to get my bags and make my bed while I could still see. Feeling the clothes that I hung on the rocks seemed to be getting dry. As I laid there I was trying to remember to find a safety pin and just how I had learned in Girl Scouts to catch fish with it. I would pray tonight that I would find one in the luggage or on some clothing. I thanked God for his provisions for most of the cases belonged to men. Thinking if I found some shaving tools they could help me if I had to scale the fish.

# Chapter 7

## What a Feast

As the light penetrated in the cave I thought today is the day I fish. I took my little flashlight and poked around in the case that I had spotted the safety pin and pulled it out. Remembering when I hung up the guys shirts I had found a couple of shirt jackets with draw strings in them. I pulled them out and tied them together and put the safety pin at the end. I found a long stick from my drift wood pile and broke off the side pieces and tied the string around the end making sure I looped it around a couple of places where I had broke off the small branch type ends.

I ate the whole mango, saving the seeds, as this morning I was really hungry. I climbed out of the cave stopping at the very top and looking with the binoculars around the shore line and the horizon. No ships so I was ready for the day of fishing. When I got back from my 'worship' rock I was ready for the challenge. I went to the grove of trees and planted the seeds, hoping those I put into the sand would harvest new ones to come up.

Trying out the strength of my tying I looped it around a rock to see if it would hold. As I bounced it up and down it held but thought I ought to tie a heavier rock and then bounced it a couple of times. I forgot the couch shell so climbed back into the cave and cut a chunk of meat out of it. Having to crush the end of the shell between two rocks made a messy sight but at least I had fish bait. I looked at the pin and bent it back using a rock and pounding at the hole where I threaded the string through, which was very hard to do. I took my cycle T-shirt and laid it along the water edge. It started to drift away so laid it on a rock that was in the water but not completely submerged and let it run down the sides. Then I threw the string out and prayed for a fish. I didn't have to wait very long to see them but they only swam around the bait and stayed near the rock where the cloth was. Finally one took the hook and I pulled but lost it. I tried again and again and thought they didn't like the bait when all of a sudden one took it and I pulled and drug it upon the shore. As I looked at it, not having any idea what kind it was or whether it was good for eating I knew God was not going to allow me to catch a dangerous type fish. Thinking it would be for a couple of meals but not wanting it to spoil I would have to eat it for lunch and supper. Getting the knife I put the fish on a large rock and cut out the stomach area and fins. I decided I would leave the head on so I could put a stick through the mouth to hold it over the fire. I remembered seeing a large flat rock down by the 'worship' rock and thought it would make a good base for my fire to sit on since the sand was damp and I wasn't sure if the fire would stay lit. Watching the horizon as I walked, I saw the rock I needed and looked and found another one so carried them both back. I left the fish on the rock by the shore and picked it up and put it on flat rock. I crawled up backwards on the boulder being careful not to drop the fish back into the sand. Letting the flat stones drop down inside I tied the fish in the tail of my shirt. Putting it on the flat rock I started stacking the wood in a small pile with the grass underneath. Using the lighters the fire started very quickly so while it was burning down to make hot coals I cut up some sticks to make smalls poles with a Y at the top and then used a thin stick and stuck it into the mouth of the fish across the top and out the back. I hung it on the Y sticks that I put in the sand and watched the fish start to cook. Taking the coconut bowls I had saved for such an occasion I chopped up chunks of papaya and mango and added them. I do not like raw fish so watched it carefully to make sure it was cooking all the way through. While it was cooking I worried about the smoke so went to the top and looked out to see if any ships had anchored way out in the ocean. Not seeing anything I went back to my cooking. I had saved some coconut oil that I used for my skin as it was easy to get sunburned even in the late morning sun. I took a piece of cloth that I had left from the T-shirts and dabbed the oil on the fish. It started to smell so great I thought I could eat it raw, but waited. Finally I laid the fish on the other flat rock I had found and took my knife and peeled back the skin. I cut a piece and ate it but only cut around the edges that I was sure was done and then laid the fish back on one of the rocks bordering the fire. I figured it could continue to cook while I ate the other pieces. I like to save the seeds and peelings from the fruit and plant in the grove of trees. It was so delicious that I wasn't sure if I was going to save any for another meal. Thinking I had better not overeat I saved the other half for supper. I left it laying on the rock until the fire went down.

The sun was high over the cave so knew it would be too hot to go up but went anyway to look around. I looked down to where I had been fishing and saw the rag that I had laid on the rock to tempt the fish. Thinking to myself, I should not have left it there in case the boat would return and see it there, so rang down to retrieve it. I rung it out and could see the fish so knew at least once a month I would eat good! I thought to myself that I was getting careless and promised myself I had to be more aware of what I was doing. My mind was getting to be very cloudy so was hoping the fish would energize me.

Climbing back into the cave I decided I needed to rest and plan my trip around the cliffs of rock to find some flint type stones to make a fire with. For me, in Girl Scouts, it was easier to use the sticks but I worried they would be too damp. I sat in the pool of water and then laid down on my 'bag' bed and fell asleep.

Waking up I looked at the opening and knew I had slept a long time and went up to look out. The sun was over to the west horizon already so knew I would not have time to look for rocks so decided that would be my adventure for tomorrow. I also wanted to take the writing tablets I found and take them out and dry them against the boulder on the ground. It was time to start journaling for too much had happened and I wanted to record it all. Knowing the military would not be looking for me any longer and now counted it to be almost 5 months living on this island. I had recorded on the briefcase and now I had run out of room. Sitting on the boulder and watching the shore line as the waves came in and out I saw that each had its own different energy. As I sat there I remember in Job where a verse asked, 'Can you raise your voice to the clouds,' and knowing I had been doing this every morning and knowing He has the wisdom to tip over the water jars of the heavens to give me the ***water of life*** I needed every day. Now the clouds were beginning to form and I saw the darkest come fast as the sun set. The wind was starting to blow pretty hard so went down to the area where I found the flat rocks and brought 2 more back. I thought if the rains got to bad I could use them to cover the hole. I carried one at a time up the boulder and then finding four heavier round type rocks to put on top of the flat ones so the wind would not blow them off the hole to the cave entrance. I laid them where the flat was tilted toward the trees so the water would run off and not back into the cave. I knew I would get some rain but the sand would soak it up fast. I sat on the boulder until the wind was so strong I needed to go down below.

I wasn't tired so thought I would see if the fire had burnt out and if not add more wood. To my amazement it still had hot coals so laid some bigger pieces on it. I put the bed near the fire and watched the flames dance and sizzle. All of a sudden I saw lightening flashes at the opening of the boulder but so thankful I was safe and dry. I couldn't hear the thunder and was happy for I never liked it. Realizing God knew this so He made this cave my fortress for now. I fell into a peaceful sleep with the warmth of the fire and the food that had filled me up.

# Chapter 8

## What is that Sparkle?

My journal was started but some of the entries would say, 'nothing different today'. I didn't want to use up valuable lines as I didn't know how long I would be there. I still had trust and faith that God was in control and he didn't save me to allow all that had happened to be in vain. I just had to wait for what he was teaching me and preparing me for. I found 3 new little sprouts coming up in the grove of papaya and mango. Not sure which they were I thanked the Lord for this would be future food if he chose for me to still be here.

I had done the regular trips around the island and now after 2 years I knew how many steps it took to go completely around. If anything on the beach was undisturbed I would notice and wonder why. After every big storm I would pick up items and carry them to the cave where I would look them over and wonder how I could use them. Last night there was a horrible storm but I wasn't sure if it was of hurricane force or not. Water spilled into the cave opening in bucketful's and I found myself sitting on the high side of the cave and thought, 'is this the way I am going to die'? It lasted for hours but was so dark I wished I could light a fire. I knew the wood would be damp even though I couldn't see to manage it. Finally the rain stopped pouring into the cave. I climbed up to see if it was light enough to climb out but it was still raining. The winds had died down for the storm was moving off to the east. The rain was warm as it always is on the island. I love to walk in the rain for it washes away the sweat and give my now long hair a good 'rain-rinse'.

The rain stopped and the sun was almost overhead and so humid now. I walked down one side of the island but it was unbearable to walk with such humidity. I noticed that a lot of sand had been washed away near one of the cliffs that had a flat side. Nothing was down at that end but rocks and the sand had washed completely to the narrow side of the island. I was looking at the cliff and something bright hit my eyes in the sand. Nothing had been that shiny before when I walked along the shore. I tried to keep my eyes on the spot but it would go away so I would step to one side and then the other trying to catch the sparkle again. When I found it I would take a few more steps each time toward it. Finally I thought I knew exactly where it was and walked over to it but saw only debris that the storm had washed up. I took one of the sticks and scraped along the sand thinking it might be a rock with glitter. I found nothing and picked up the drift wood pieces and carried them back to the boulder. The sun was beating down and I was sweating up a storm. I knew this was not good for I needed all the moister in my body since I was eating more fish.

I went down into the cave and proceeded to write a little more in the journal about the storm and the pretty sparkle on the beach. I read over the last few pages to see if I left anything out and was amazed to remember the ships coming and going but never encountering them again for I played it safe when I saw the ship I stayed below for a couple of days. I saw things in the water that told me it looked like the package that I had found but I never went out in the water to pick it up. They seemed to stay in the same area from the shore and I felt relieved it didn't come on shore.

Keeping the flat rocks off the opening I knew the sun and breeze would blow into the cave and take out the high humidity in a few days. Mastering the fire making technique with pieces of flint I could light one in a few days to help take out some of the dampness I thought.

I notice my skin was cracking pretty bad and felt I needed to put something on besides coconut oil. I took the skins of the papaya and mango and scraped the inside and put it in one of my coconut bowls. Smashing them together I added a little oil until it was smooth I figured I would put it on one arm. If it was not good and I broke out in a rash I sure wouldn't put it on any other part of my body. I was wearing the long sleeved white shirts that were in the duffle bags. There were also some dark jockey shorts so tore them to where I could make a wrap around my arm. As much as I sweat I knew the mixture would not stay on or soak up into the sleeves of the shirt at night. This was the only way I could think to help it stay on my skin. That night I sat on the boulder looking around as the sun was going down watching the horizon and lathered the mixture on my arm. Wow! It sure smelt good, good enough to eat!! I started to climb down and noticed the rope was fraying so I laid there in bed trying to think of how to protect the rope when it rubbed on the edge of the rock as I went up and down. Project for tomorrow I thought and fell into a peaceful sleep again.

After eating more fruit for breakfast I climbed up cautiously and went down to pray and sing. On the way back I decided to check out the area where I saw the shiny object. Rounding the corner of the cliff there it was shining as before. I don't always take the binoculars with me but this morning I did. The calendar showed it had been about 6 weeks since I saw the box in the water off shore. So taking the binoculars and looking at the object I followed its trail a little better. Stepping from side to side until I picked it up but this time I noticed what debris it was near and walked to it. Kneeling down I took a stick and started raking the sand. Back and forth, back and forth and when I went farther toward the cliff my stick stopped on something that was sticking out of the sand. Crawling to it I took my hands and brushed the sand away from it and to my surprise it shined like gold. I got so excited that I was not looking out to sea and continued to dig around the object. When I got about 12 inches down there were bright colored stones up and down and it looked like it might be a cane or something. I was breathing pretty hard and sat back to stare at the object, then glanced out to the sea and saw the large ship sitting where it normally does. I quickly sunk a stick into the sand where the object was and covered it up. Crawling low, I looked with the binoculars but could not see if the little boat was coming, I quickly climbed up on the boulder and slid down not raising up at all. I hesitated for I had forgotten to rake the sand with the palm branch and left it lying where I had been digging. I prayed that God would bring a stronger breeze to cover my footprints. I didn't want to hang on the rope for it was getting weak so went down into the cave and stayed there for that day.

As I lay on my bed I was trying to think of anything I might have seen in books that might have those types of stones on. I imagined pirates hiding buried treasure there many years ago maybe. I couldn't wait to investigate tomorrow when ship was gone.

It was too early to go to bed for the night as light was still coming in the cave. I got out my journal and just sat in the shadow of the sun and wrote of my findings. I was looking at the heavy jackets I had laid in my bed and thought these would make strong support pieces to wrap the rope in that was fraying. I wished now I had some of that duck tape that was on that package but figured the material would work too. One of the airmen's fatigue pants were still hanging on the wall of the cave so thought if I could rip strips from the leg and then wrap it around the rope it would last for a while. Putting it into the sun spot I proceeded to tear the pant leg. Climbing the rope had weakened my wrist so found the knife to cut the material. I could wrap it between the two knots and secure it by tying more material to keep it from slipping down. I will do that in the morning if the ship is gone. I was bothered by the weakness of my wrist so decided I was going to have to find something to grip like a tennis ball. Sure there must be one around here somewhere!!! I got in the pool and soaked as I had worked up a sweat digging and felt relaxed in the water. I took a couple of the white shirts in with me and washed them at the edge where the water was flowing down into the side of the cliff. I would take them out in the morning and let the wind fluff them up for me. I decided to climb up and peek out to see if I saw anything and was horrified to see a fire going near my little cave. I didn't notice any people for I ducked down seeing the fire. Maybe as dusk settles in they would not be able to see me for I had put the rocks around the opening to hide my head. I figured it had to be the men from the big ship for the small boat shows up soon after spotting it. Just who are these men?

Waiting long enough I thought I would climb back up and saw it was almost dark but the fire was still going. I laid my head against the opening and listened for voices. I heard glass breaking and laughter but still could not understand what they were saying. I decided it was too dangerous for me to be too noisy and it was not worth getting spotted. I climbed down and lay down on my bed. Praying for safety I fell asleep. That is one thing my father God was so good at doing was quieting my spirit to rest in Him and know he was taking the night watch for me.

Morning came and I hurried to the top to see if the men were still on the beach. Much to my disappointment they were laying on the sand asleep. Guess they had drank a lot so was sleeping it off. I looked out and saw the ship still in the same place so knew they were waiting on these men, but what were they waiting on, I thought.

I cut myself some more mangos and ate a couple of chunks of coconut for breakfast. If the ship left today I needed to fish as it had been a month since my last tasty batch. Not feeling the best this morning I was alright with the men being there for that gave me the excuse to rest. I lay in my bed and surprisingly I fell back to sleep. Waking with the sun shining on me from the cave opening I knew it was high noon. I jumped up and climbed to peer out carefully and first noticed the men were not on the sand. I turned to see if their boat was in the deep area and it had gone. Glancing closer to the shore I saw the boat going out to sea and figured they were going back to the ship. Thanking God that he kept me safe once more I climbed down to wait for the big ship to leave.

Today I would fix the rope and make it sturdier so it would not break and drop me to the bottom. I know twelve feet isn't a long way and I would land on the sand. I rolled the strips of material in a ball to have it ready and tore some short ones for tying. I then wrote in the journal. I could just hear the girls as they would read my notes and that is why I wanted to document it all. Never a day went by that I did not think of them and all the experiences we had that were instrumental in my staying alive.

My thoughts went to thinking that Donny would be graduating this year and going off to college and hopefully getting a sport scholarship. I was so proud of all his achievements in school and his Christian walk. He loved working with kids in the neighborhood with T-ball and football.

Becky loved sports too so I wasn't sure what her future was going to be. She loved helping me in girl scouts and having friends over a lot. It was never unusual to see her walking home from school with a group walking with her. She was full of life and a joy to watch her grow.

Bonnie was my quiet one but also involved in sports and was a Brownie Girl Scout. Seemed she would sit back and listen to her older sister and brother just learning to where she would fit in as she grew older and became her own self. I kept her close to me and enjoyed this little girl who seemed to like her independence.

As I laid there thinking about them and wondering what they would be doing I broke down and cried with longing to hold them and tell them I loved them. Many a morning I would scream, when I was at my 'rock', their names calling to them, 'I am alive, please wait for me, and don't forget me.' I did feel Donny would go on to college and I wanted to be there for Becky to help her decide what she wanted to do. I prayed to God to let me be rescued so I wouldn't miss their young adult life for this was an important age to have the support of their parents. With Brad gone all the time I was hoping the government would not let him go on so many TDY trips now that he was a single dad. I knew God would hear my desires so I rested in his arms and fell asleep.

Realizing I must have drifted off I jumped up and climbed to look out into the sea where the large ship was and to my excitement it was gone. I knew I had to work on the rope because climbing up just now 2 strands of rope broke off. I sat on the boulder and wound the strips of cloth around the rope. I pulled it tight after each turn and then holding the knot in my mouth tied the top just above the knot real tight. Turning sideways I did the same for the top section just under the knot where the fraying was worse. I saw that the rock it had been sliding on was rough. I got down finding a sharp sided rock that would make the rock smooth.

I jumped down and walked over to where the men had made a fire. The sound of breaking glass was their booze bottles which they had thrown against the outside of the small cave. I knew I would have to clean it up, for if I had to go into there on an emergency, I would cut my legs up bad. I found two nice size pieces that I thought would cut up my fruit and fish. Also it would be good for anything that I didn't have to cut. They were raw cut all around and I had to be careful I didn't cut my palm using them. Where is that duct tape???

Nothing else had been left on the sand except the burnt wood. That was MY WOOD that I had saved and was drying against the boulder. OK, fair trade .... wood for the money!!! Now I don't feel bad in keeping it. I needed to take the seeds to the mango grove and plant them so walked down and picked 2 more for my meals.

I decided to walk around the island since I had not done it for a couple of days with my visitors there. They must have found most of the drift wood for I didn't find any to use. As I was walking back to the cave I remembered I had been digging for buried treasure!!! Walking up the beach I saw something long and white floating in the water. I waded out to see what it was and it looked like a piece of foam and just the right size for a mattress. Hard but better than the bumpy bag of clothes I was laying on. I carried it back and dropped it down into the cave. It was exactly two feet wide so pushing it down was easy. I went back to the area I had been digging in and was thankful the stick was still visible to see. Once again I started pushing the sand away from the gold piece and it seemed the more I dug the longer it was. It only had 5 jewel stones that were red, green, purple and white. Looking at the side of the object it had a handle type below the stones. I kept digging and my hands and fingers were getting sore but couldn't think of what I had to help me dig. I started digging on one side down but it wouldn't budge. As I got about 12 inches down I thought to myself this looked like a dagger or sword handle. I was getting really excited and knew I had to keep digging. The sun was dropping fast so I turned around and started pushing the sand away with my feet. I stood up and started pushing the object back and forth pulling up when finally with the last pull it gave way and came out. It sat me down on the ground pretty hard. In my hand was a 2 foot sword of brilliant gold for there was not one stone gone. I couldn't believe my eyes. Where and who did this belong to I thought. Did I really find a pirates treasure . . . . was there more in this hole? As I made my way to the cave I decided I was going to build me a fire for I knew the men would not be back this quick. I hurried down for the light was almost gone and I would be able to see to start the fire. I put the flat stone near the light that penetrated the cave and worked at lighting the grass and then small sticks and carried it over to the pile of larger wood. It didn't take long to get a roaring fire and it lit up the cave in a warm and relaxing way. I laid my new bed over by the fire and sat there with the sword lying beside me rubbing it and feeling like I had a secret and couldn't tell anyone.

I ate some more fruit and coconut and enjoyed the fresh water that flowed from the spring into the pool. Amazing that it was cool and yet it was so hot outside. Where did it come from? Only God knew, for he provided it for me. I laid down watching the stones on the sword glow from the fire. Talking to the sword and asked it if it had lots of stories to tell! I would love to know who it was made for. I fell asleep waking up once to put more wood on the fire and then it was morning.

# Chapter 9

# Becky, Need Help in Braiding

My borrowed clothes were wonderful as they were big and baggy for I was getting very skinny but it made them cooler to wear. With my hair getting long I needed to tie it back but couldn't find any cloth that kept it up and out of my face unless I tied it from the back to the top. I decided I would try my skill at braiding. I know there was some tall grass that grew around the orchard area so maybe I could use them. I knew I had to braid them while they were green or they would tear or break. I remembered when my Becky told the younger girl scouts this when they were learning to make belts out of the reeds along the shore of the lake we were camping at.

I decided after I went to my 'rock' I would go by the grass area where the reeds were and take my knife to cut them. So eating some fruit I walked down and prayed to the Lord in praise and singing. Going by the reeds I cut a dozen long pieces and carried them back to the cave. As I sat against the large boulder in the shade I found it was hard to keep it braided so used two rocks, one on top of the other and putting the reed under it like a clamp. In scouts they used the buddy system but I had none!! It was not as easy as I thought, for it was cutting my hands. I knew if I got an infection it would be hard to heal. Thinking if I kept them wet, it would soften them so I took them down into the cave and laid them in the pool.

Before the sun got any hotter, I would do some fishing for I was getting hungry and the fruit I had eaten the last couple of weeks was not enough. I planned on eating one fish three times a week but the fish were tired of the couch meat, so if I got one per week I knew it was because the Lord was blessing me. Certain times of the month I knew I needed to eat more I usually stayed in bed for at least 3 days. It would be easy to catch a fish and hopefully to get a couple and keep it in a spot I dug at the end of the spring that went into the cave wall. I had to build rocks around it before it went down into the rock, otherwise not being salt water, it would not last long. I didn't stay out too long before I had two fish so joyfully knew I would eat well for lunch and supper.

The sun was now over head so I was glad to get the fire going again for eating this time. Making my usual meal, that always tasted great, I thanked God for his provisions as always. I cleaned up my mess and relaxed on the foam bed. Maybe after my nap I would start on the reeds and try to braid them.

I thought about doing some more digging but while I was trying to think of what I could use I drifted off. I woke up and noticed it was dusk again. I am sleeping longer during the day now but it is not bothering my sleeping at night. I knew my body was beginning to wear down. I decided I had to eat fish at least 3 times a week like I had planned. My body was so thin I knew I didn't have much fat to live off anymore.

Taking the reeds out of the water I thought I will give this a try but they came to pieces so knew they must be the wrong kind of reed. I was braiding my hair but with nothing to keep them tied up they just fell lose after a while.

# Chapter 10

# Lord, Let Them Be My Rescuers

I am finding after almost 3 years now I will never be saved. I want to believe you Lord but I can't even climb out of the cave but twice a day now. I don't have the strength to light a fire much anymore. I sleep all the time so what am I good for Lord? I started crying and just couldn't stop. I knew I had to climb out of the cave to get some fruit and I had no more fish left so that will be all the strength I can do today. I started the fire for I really had to have some fish today. After slipping a couple of times I knew it wouldn't be long before I would not be able to pull myself up. Maybe I would have to move back into my small cave and live in the raft.

Using each rock that stuck out of the cave wall near the rope was the only way I could pull myself up. My hands were boney so had to wrap them in cloth so the skin would not break and bleed. I lay down on the top and was sliding down the rock so I wouldn't fall. I fell, as usual to the sand and sat there resting before getting up. As I walked to the grove of trees I heard a buzzing motor sound. It would cut in and out so kept looking at the ocean for the boat to return. I was too far from the big or little cave so rushed to the grove and laid down amongst the trees looking everywhere in the water for a boat. Then out of the corner of my eye I looked up and saw a helicopter . . . . no, two of them flying over to the far end of the island where it was all open. They landed behind the cliff so I ran and hide behind it peering around it to see what kind of helicopter it was. As I read US ARMY on the side and the emblem of the star I started crying and crawling to them. I was half walking and half crawling waving my arms as they were looking at the helicopter. They looked down the beach but not in my direction and I knew they couldn't hear me screaming over the engine noise. I did a brazen thing and took off my white shirt and started waving it. This caught the eye of one of the pilots and he started walking toward me. I quickly pulled the shirt back on crying so hard I couldn't stand up. There were 4 men and they all ran to me. I told them I was an Air Force dependent marooned on the island after the plane took off from Guam AFB and it went down 3 years ago. They picked me up and carried me to the helicopter. I was hugging the pilot and crying, 'thank you' over and over. He kept telling me I was going to be fine and they would take me home. Listening to them talk they had a decision now as the helicopter only held 4 people and they were going to fly to get parts and come back. I told them it wouldn't be safe to leave the plane there because of the bad guys coming to the island a lot. They talked it over and called on the radio of their position and trouble. They couldn't get a response but kept trying. One of the pilots got out a map of the ocean islands but could not even find this island on it. Two of the pilots decided to take off and fly till they got reception and tell their Commander of the situation. Then they would come back. The other two told them they needed to get the parts and to go on. I wanted to get my I.D. card and things from the cave so told them I had a suitcase that had items belonging to some of the crew that went down with the plane. I told them how and why I had brought them on the raft. Some of them were duffle bags and briefcases so kept some of the personal items to take back to the families. They said of course so they helped me walk to the cave and they climbed down with me. I dug up the leather duffle type bag while the other two were trying to focus on the cave and the way I had to live. I wrapped some of the clothes around the sword but did not tell the guys I had found it or the money. I took the 3 pretty shells, one for each girl and handed it to one of the pilots. Thankful the fire was still going I went over and put more on so they could see the cave. One of the soldiers started crying and again asked me, 'how long have you been here"? I took the briefcase to him where I had marked the outside and then showed him my journal and how I marked it so we could see the dates of how long I had lived here. We all climbed back to the top and they walked me to the other helicopter. I told the pilots, how to look out of the cave every morning and look for the large ship. This would tell them they were going to get visited by some mean men who killed and if they saw the helicopter they would certainly come looking for you. I'd be afraid they would call to the big ship and they might bomb the island. I laughed and said I watched war movies with my husband. They laughed too but it could be the truth. I found out they were stationed at Guam so knew who to contact in getting me help. Leaving the other two men behind I hugged them both and said I would be praying for their safety and for the quick return of parts. They promised to come and visit me for they were sure I would have to go to the hospital first.

I was so thankful to God for I was finally rescued and flying back to be with my family. I started crying and one of the pilots reached his hand out to me and patted my leg. They put one of the helmets on me so we could talk back and forth. One was Major Davidson and the other Captain Carroll but I didn't know their first names. I leaned against the seat and looked out the window but could not see anything. They were not able to get communication around the island and couldn't understand why. It took several hours before we were landing at Guam. As we landed and the engine died down the door opened and their waiting for me was a wheel chair. My legs were so weak I was grateful that they thought of that. I was put in the back of an emergency military wagon reminding the guys to please come and see me and they promised they would see me in the morning. I started crying again for I was scared to death to be alone but knowing I was on US soil it was tears of thanksgiving.

We pulled up to the emergency door of the hospital at Guam and two men in medic uniforms came running out and wheeled me into an exam room. I kept telling them to get my bag for I had my I.D. card and things in there for my family and the families of the crash victims. They put my bag under the exam table. Then they started with all the procedures of admitting me, taking my card to get all the information about me from the DEERS Program that they had started. I asked one if I could just take a shower and go to bed tonight. They said I would have to wait until the doctor came in but they were sure it would be fine. I laid my head on the table while sitting in the wheel chair and cried for I was so cold and shivering badly. Not being used to the air-conditioning they thought I was going into shock so picked me up and laid me on the exam bed. I just said I was so cold. As the doctor came in they were carrying blankets and wrapped me in them. The sergeant told the doctor what I wanted to do so he sat down and told me he had to ask me some questions about what the pilots had told him. When I told him of the crash and how long I had been on the island he just sat there and stared at me. He then got up and told the sergeant to take me to a room and get me some clean clothes to put on after I showered. Then he turned around and said I will be up to your room and ask you just a few more questions and save the rest for tomorrow. He wanted to get started locating Brad and the girls for he said they were no longer stationed there.

I think I must have been in the shower 15 minutes but washing all my hair it took a lot of shampoo and then to rinse it out. They had put a chair in there for me and I was so thankful. I was just too weak to stand. Drying off and putting on a hospital gown I went out to where a nurse was fixing my bed. She told me her name was Mary and asked if there was anything I wanted. I was shivering and my teeth were chattering so bad that I almost couldn't answer her. I did ask her for some warm blankets and maybe some warm tea. When she got back I was laying in the bed all curled up and had almost fallen asleep but sat up to accept the tea and she wrapped me in the warm blankets. It felt so good and I started crying again. She sat on the bed and rubbed my arm and told me that I was in good hands and she would be a 'push of the button away'. I could hear her ask me questions but just couldn't concentrate to answer. I said, 'I'm sorry, I am so tired I can't think straight.' The doctor came in and told me he had called the base locator to find Brad and they had gone back to our old base. I knew this would make the children happy for we had been there longer than any other base. He said it was after hours so would have to contact the base during working hours. Taking the empty cup from me he had me lay down and Mary came over and tucked me in all around and said to sleep well. I was so exhausted from the days capture. Thanking the Lord I fell into a deep sleep for it was day light when I opened my eyes. At first I forgot where I was for I thought I was dreaming. I sat up and realized I needed to go to the bathroom so with one leg at a time I stood beside the bed. Walking was painful but made it and back before anyone came to check on me.

I buzzed the nurse and another one came in smiling and patting my arm. She said the doctor was on his way and he would be telling them the next step in helping me. No sooner had she said it than the doctor, I had met last night, was at the foot of the bed. He knew I had a good night's sleep for it was recorded I didn't move all night and laughed. I was being told they would be coming to take some blood just to see where to start as I needed nourishment and they would probably want to do it with an IV. He asked me what all I ate on the island and knew I wouldn't be able to handle solid food yet. For now I was to rest and when he reviewed the tests he would be back. He said there would be someone from the Champus office to come and talk to me and help me to locate my family. I was told I could have some more tea and I could have some Jell-O for breakfast. Yippee! Something different.

In between taking blood from me and sleeping most of the day it was evening. I was brought a cup of tea by one of the pilots who had rescued me. He hugged me and sat on the bed and said I could call him Will. He was from Iowa and had a little girl 7 and boy 3. He would be going to Ft.

Hood in Texas in a month. He and Captain Carroll would be flying out in the morning to pick up the other two pilots and repair the helicopter. Not understanding why, they still could not communicate with them so wanted to get there as soon as possible. He said his goodbye and would be back in 2 days. I prayed for all of them to arrive back here safely.

Whatever they were feeding me I was beginning to have a clearer vision and things didn't look so fuzzy. That evening my doctor, Major Phillips came in to see if there was anything I needed before he left for the day. I asked him if there was any word about my family and he said he had not but was busy trying to find a doctor who specialized in getting me on my feet. He was gone and I looked out the window at my surroundings but only saw a parking lot with some cars in it. Wow, how long had it been since I saw that sight.

# Chapter 11

# Off Again

Morning came, with the business of nurses and technicians doing their usual blood taking. I asked one if I had any left or did they have to wait overnight so I would make more!! He explained the more they could find out the sooner they could start helping me. I told him all I needed was food to build me up and a cream to clear up my sun sores. I didn't get a response so wondered why so much attention with my blood.

Hallelujah! After they got through with taking blood they said I would get oatmeal this morning!! It tasted so good and I asked for more. The nurse said let's give it an hour or so and then see if you can have more. My tummy had shrunk, I was sure, so did not want to make myself sick. I got up and took a shower but didn't wash my hair this time. They had given me lots of lotions to lather all over me for my skin was so dry and scaly that it took a lot to soak in. At first on the island the coconut did fine but it took a lot and I didn't have enough to do all the time.

Dr Phillips came in and said they were going to transport me to Hickam AFB in Hawaii tomorrow for they found a doctor who specialized in tropical blood problems. I told him, 'if he is a man of God then God will show him, so when do I leave'? He smiled and agreed that God is the Great Physician and he leans on His wisdom all the time. Reaching over he patted my hand and told me he would be back. I started praying that this new doctor would indeed know what to do for I wanted to get back to my family as soon as they fix me. I must be taking in fluid and nutrients by the gallons for I just kept using the bathroom, but I knew that was a good thing! It showed my kidneys still worked great. Thank you Lord.

On the fifth day I was told I would be getting dressed to go. I mentioned to the nurse that all I had was a couple of men's shirts to wear so could I borrow some surgery clothes. She went down and brought me a pair of them with a top and bottom that were PINK. I then told her I also had nothing to wear under them. She quickly disappeared and came back after about an hour with a bra and panties. Now I felt like a lady again! I got my shower over and they disconnected my IV and we waited for the plane to take me to Hickam. Meanwhile I asked Mary if she would contact the pilots and told her their names to relay the message that I was leaving. About 30 minutes later the four of them walked in my room AND of course I started crying. They said they had just got back last night and would have come over but by the time they debriefed it was too late. Major Davidson said they had a tough time finding the island so had to fly low, almost on top of the water, to find it. I asked if they got visited by the bad guys and they said, no. I praised the Lord right then for I sure didn't want them to get hurt. Major Davidson came over and handed me an envelope and said the guys in the squadron took up a donation for me so that I would have money now until the government could help me out. As we were talking Mary came in with one of the medic corpsman and said it was time to leave. I thanked them, for now they would be part of my life forever and I didn't want to loose contact with them. The pilots all said they would keep in contact and Captain Carroll promised he would come when he got to Hickam to bring in his family. I was so happy and looked forward to knowing I knew someone there. I tucked the envelope in my bag and they wheeled me out.

As they were driving me to the flight line I saw one of the planes that I went down in coming closer and we drove toward it. I started saying, 'oh no, oh no'. One of the Sergeants asked me what was wrong and I told him that is like the plane I went down in. He reassured me it would be fine. I just whispered, 'Okay Lord, it's your watch again and I am in your hands as always'. They carried me on and strapped me in all the while talking and laughing to me. I know they were trying to relax me. I ask the Lord to just let me sleep during the whole flight . . . AND HE DID!

I woke as the plane was landing and praised the Lord for His continued protection for me. There were several military men on the plane just like before but as we came to a halt I was taken out first and again was met by an ambulance with a wheel chair. Watching them as they carried my bag I asked them if I could just carry it on my lap. One of the crewmen gave it to the Sergeant in the ambulance. I thanked them all and said my goodbyes.

They took me directly to the base hospital and put me in a room where there were two beds. I took the bed by the window and when I looked out I saw it looked over a courtyard type area. A nurse came in and said she was

Donna and would be my day time nurse. I got into those wonderful gowns and lay back waiting for what was to come. She left the room so I got my journal out of my bag and decided to start writing what had taken place so far. I pulled the table up across my bed and began.

# Chapter 12

# Meeting My New Doctor

Just as I got my pencil to start writing a bald headed nice looking doctor, who looked to be my age, walked in and just stood staring at me. He was in uniform so knew he was military or a reservist and clip board in his hand. I felt he might be a doctor or lab technician looking me over. I looked back and said, 'Hi'! He said, 'Hello, are you Lucinda?' I said, 'yes'. He continued looking at me and then to the clip board and said, 'I have questions to ask you.' Responding, I said, 'okay have a seat', pointing to the foot of my bed, and I took my journal off my table and said, 'you can use my table'. Smiling he said, 'thank you', with a question in his voice. I then asked, 'and you are . . . . ?' Looking upset that I should have known, he said, 'I'm Lieutenant Colonel Hartman, your doctor'. I smiled and stretched out my hand and said, 'oh, great, I'm glad to meet you'.

He looked at the clipboard then asked me my full name and address! I didn't say anything but just laughed and said, 'well, I guess the hospital's'. 'Oh, yeah', he said in agreement. 'Your phone number . . . .' no, this form is useless!' He walked out. I started laughing for I had not seen a doctor become flustered asking me questions. He came back in a couple of minutes and said, 'Let's do this again'. And we both started laughing. I said, 'would you like for me to fill that out and I could have the nurse come and get it when I was done'? He looked at me and then responded, 'Do you mind?' I will come back and finish your exam when I have something to go on. I could see him breathe a sigh of relief. I worked on the forms that were so familiar that I couldn't understand why he was nervous over it. I buzzed Donna and she came and got it. I asked her who he was and she said, he is the hospital commander but specializes in tropical diseases. So I asked her if I had a disease. Her response was that any time the military guys are stationed in tropical areas they come back with things that take special care. Wow! I have the commander taking care of me! Why did he get flustered? Maybe it was because I was a dependent woman and not a guy. But women go to those places too. Oh, well I will just have to ask him questions when he has seen my blood work.

Later that day I got a visit from my commander Doctor Hartman. He was just stopping by to say goodnight and he would be talking to me in the morning about all the blood work results that had been done already at Guam. He said in the morning I wasn't going to be able to eat for he needed some more blood drawn. The night nurse, Nancy, brought me some soup and jell-o to get me through the night. It was great to have a TV in my room and be able to watch the news. I was surprised at what was going on in the world. As Donna came in to say good night she told me she had a neighbor lady who was my size and maybe she had some clothes that would fit me. I was so grateful to know I would have something besides surgery clothes to wear and thankful for them. She asked if there was anything I needed. Knowing that I needed everything a woman needs I asked her if she could take me to the Base Exchange so I could buy some personal items? She said she would ask the doctor if I could go out of the hospital.

I awoke to a male technician standing by the bed. He said he had come to get some blood and then I would be able to have breakfast. After he was done I got up and took my shower before my breakfast arrived. Looking out my window I thought, 'I miss my worship rock' but thankful I am alive and can praise the Lord anywhere.

Donna came in full of smiles and brought my breakfast of oatmeal and toast. Even a cup for tea and orange juice! I felt weak but good. Dr Hartman had not started his rounds yet but she told me I was his only one for now. Being the Commander of the hospital his work was mainly administration and a few cases when they were full. I asked Donna for some paper to write my 'shopping' list on. She returned with a tablet and pen so I got busy. I knew I had money but wanted to go to the Credit Union to get a deposit box to put my money in, plus the items I had brought for the families including, the sword. I would later see if I could get help in locating those families.

# Chapter 13

# How Did I Get Them?

As I walked to the window and watched the birds gathering food I thought that I missed so much for I didn't have any birds, animals or snakes on the island. Thankful for that I thought, since I did not like snakes. I tapped on the window and one of the birds landed on the sill and just looked at me. Thinking I would save some of my toast tomorrow and go outside and feed them, my doctor walked in. He came over to the window and I shared how I didn't have birds on the island so missed them. I sat on the side of the bed and he sat in a chair with my records in hand. 'This is what we are going to do. Tomorrow I will start antibiotics and they will be strong and see how the parasites take to it,' he said. 'Parasites, how did they get in me?' I asked. He explained that through what I ate or if I went barefooted, it could have been anything. Continuing he said that we don't want them to invade your organs and the sooner we get you started the better. He took my hand and said, 'You are on my watch so I am here until we send you home all cleared.' As I looked at him he seemed to know what I was going to say and as I replied, 'My Lord will direct you for He is also on watch for my care.' I noticed his eyes got watery and he said, 'Indeed, He is the Captain of this ship.'

I asked him about shopping and he said, 'Yes, you can go shopping for what you need while you're here. Go over the list with Donna and she can tell you what we can get for you through the hospital'. He said as he left, 'Good luck and happy shopping'.

Donna came in and said that one of the doctor's wives had volunteered to take me shopping. She and I went over my list and we took a couple of things off mine. The hospital had very rich lotions for healing and I was allowed to use those. Donna said that Heather and her husband were friends with Dr Hartman and visited with him last night at his home and he shared all about me. I was pleased that I would get to know more people and they wanted to help.

Right after lunch I was visited by Heather Connors. Her husband, Major Perry Connors, also a doctor, works with Dr Hartman. She loved to volunteer at the hospital so was excited when Donna called her and told her of my needs and was happy to help me. So off we went to the Base Exchange. I wasn't sure if I could use my ID card anymore so we went to the manager and she told us that Colonel Hartman had already called and I could buy anything I needed.

It was so much fun for the two of us as we laughed at how women need these items to be women!! I first told her I needed a suitcase for the one small duffle bag was moldy smelling and I needed a larger one. So I loaded up the suitcase with cosmetics, clothing, pajamas and bathrobe, shoes for I needed walking shoes and sandals. She invited me to go to the Chapel with them so needed a dress, skirt, blouse and slacks. Thinking of walking I wanted shorts and a shirt. As I was just looking for necessities Heather told me that the Wives Club wanted to adopt me and help me get a wardrobe of clothing. I hugged her crying and told her to thank everyone. I felt so great knowing I had clothes and I could soon feel like a lady again and not have to wear men's shirts. On the way back to the hospital I told her I wanted to stop at the Credit Union and put the money the pilots had given me into a checking account. Also, I thought I might as well get a safety deposit box. I saw her look at the bag as we entered and I am sure she thought it was funny that I carried it in the bag so told her the items for the families of the crew were in it. That seemed to satisfy her and we walked in for I did not want anyone to know about the $250,000 and the beautiful sword that I had found, for a while anyway.

We arrived back at the hospital and I took my things to my room, Heather went with me and wanted me to meet her husband. I was so very tired but went with her and found Major Connors had a patient so we went back to the room. I was glad for I put my things in my closet and lay down on the bed. I fell asleep in no time but was awaken by Donna bringing me some soup and crackers for lunch. She said I would be hooked on an IV for food supplements and antibiotics. I ate the soup and crackers and decided I would exchange my new things into my new suitcase. Taking the items from the crew out and laying them on the window sill to air out I wanted to look for information as to how I could find the families to help the Air Force locator office. I decided to keep the papers with the names of the crew in the duffle bag. I did not want my new things to get smelly, but needed to get a zippered folder and get rid of the smelly bag. I no sooner had all the things laid out when Donna came in to put in my IV. Dr Hartman was right behind her. He came over to the window and asked what they were and I told him. Both he and Donna got very teary eyed and both put there arms around me and said they would help if I needed them. Dr Hartman asked me how my shopping trip went and I laughed and said, 'Great!' He was polite but stated Heather had offered last night when they visited him. I thanked him for suggesting Heather for she was very sweet person. He said they did not have children so she volunteers a lot to help others.

As he and Donna got me hooked up he said I should rest now since I had a full morning of 'women' shopping. We both laughed and I commented that it was a 'girl-thing'! I drifted off to sleep and didn't wake up until Donna was at my bedside telling me good night for she was on her way home. I asked her where she lived and she said her husband worked on the flight line and lived on base. They have one little girl 3 years old. I asked her if she would bring her some week-end when they are running around. She promised she would. I told her I missed my kids and hoped that someone had news for me soon. Nancy came in to check to see how I was doing and to see if I needed anything. You would think I hadn't slept any that day for I was looking so forward to turning out the lights and going to sleep. As I looked out my window I said to myself that I was going to venture out tomorrow if at all possible to visit the birds and feed them.

I woke up a few times during the night as Nancy fiddled with my IV but smiled and drifted back to sleep. She was so quiet but I am not a sound sleeper so any noise would wake me. However, at 11:00 she came in with another nurse, male, and showed him what was going on. I said hello to him and he kind of waved back. He came in at five to take my vitals and was gone. Didn't see much of him but asked Donna the next morning what his name was and she said Todd. She said I could not have a shower this morning because of the IV in me. She brought me my usual oatmeal, toast and juice, along with a nice cup of tea. Remembering to save a slice of toast I wrapped it in my napkin. I got up and went to the bathroom and sponged off brushing my teeth and my hair. I was so excited to be able to use ties for my hair and climbed back into bed, dragging the IV 'tower'. I braided my hair to get it out of my face and got out my new notebook for my journal.

# Chapter 14

# The Call I Had Longed For

In the mid morning I had a visitor. I was writing and I looked up to have my doctor and another officer walk in. Dr Hartman introduced him as the Base Commander General Bradley and he was going to help me locate Brad and start some communication with him. He said so far Brad would not return his calls when he told him why he was calling. Finally Brad's commanding officer put in a conference call with he and Brad on the line to the General. Brad told him that he did not want to get the kids hopes built up if I might die. General Bradley told him if he had to go to his base commander and order him to tell his kids he would do it. He said, 'I also told him, you don't want me coming over there and do it, I am sure'. Commander Allen, Brad's commander, said it would not be necessary for he would handle it at that end. General Bradley assured me that I would be getting a phone call from Brad or one of the kids within the next few days or he would call Brad's commander and fly over there. I was crying by now, really big sobs, and General Bradley sat on the bed and held me saying, 'We are here for you, for what all you have gone through. We owe you!! I asked him if he knew anything about the kids and he said Brad had remarried 3 months after my disappearance. Also he said that the two older kids were married. I was now in shock that I buried my body in my bed and curled up in a fetal position and couldn't stop crying. I must have cried myself to sleep for when I woke Donna was sitting at the foot of the bed with a Bible in her hand. I sat up and she held out a cold wet cloth and I started crying again. She came closer and put her arms around my shoulders and handed me the Bible. She told me she had turned it to Psalm 23 and wanted to read it to me. As she read I knew God was in control and just to have this young lady know Him too reassure me of the Comforter who came through her to give me peace of heart. As we sat there another officer walked in and he introduced himself as Chaplain Fergus and wanted to pray with me. He said Colonel Hartman had called and wanted the Bible Study groups to pray for me. He wanted to come and meet me personally and affirm that the Lord was with me.

Two days later I received a call from Brad in my room. He started off by telling me we were not getting back together for he had remarried and wanted to stay married to her. I was told by General Bradley I would have to be the one to get the divorce. I told Brad I would divorce him after the government assured me of my benefits that were due me. I have seven years before I could legally be confirmed dead. Brad started swearing at me and told me he would never let me see the kids if I did not divorce him right away. I told him I would have to get a lawyer and see what my options were. I needed the military benefits for my medical care right now. He slammed the phone down so I called General Bradley and he said he would handle it by getting the base advocate to look into our situation.

I went down to the chapel area in the hospital and just sat talking to the Lord for I needed him to give me direction to what I needed. I knew if the military wouldn't allow me to have medical benefits I did have the money to go to a civilian hospital. Maybe this is why the Lord allowed me to find the money. So many questions and I just needed the Lord to help me know what to do. I must have been down there for an hour when I heard my name paged to return to my room. As I walked in General Bradley was there with the base's legal advocate for military personnel. He told me legally he could not help me as Brad was the military person involved here. General Bradley told me he had called a personal lawyer friend that would help me. The advocate did advise me on several issues that I would face but General Bradley assured me I would win. I couldn't believe these folks here at Hickam were so caring about me even if it wasn't protocol. It can only be done through God's people and him directing them. Dr Hartman mentioned after General Bradley left my room the other day that if the government won't help this woman then I may retire. I am going to do what I can for her, she didn't do anything wrong and it was our plane she was flying in.

I spent the rest of the day pretty much alone. I think everyone knew what had happened and didn't know what to say to me so avoided coming in. Donna brought my lunch and said if I needed to talk to buzz her. Heather called and told me Major Connors had called her to get the prayer chain working at the Chapel and be praying for wisdom. I thanked her for she too said she would be volunteering tomorrow and would be by to visit.

I tried to rest after I ate lunch but my mind hurt too much to relax. Reminding the Lord I had faith and trust in what was happening but my mind was on the kids and wanting to see them so bad. I walked out to the courtyard with some cracker crumbs and enjoyed the fresh air. Hearing my name, I turned around and there was Dr Hartman asking me if I was alright. He said that everyone told him to tell me they were praying for me. Tears rolled down my face as I thanked him and then he said he was leaving to go work out at the gym.

I woke up to the sound of rain out my window. It was early so I got up and showered, dressed in surgery clothes, made up my bed and went quietly down to the hospital chapel area. No one comes in early and very few during the day but I am thankful they have this private area just to talk to the Lord without interruptions. I always left a note on my table if they needed me right away.

It was time for shift change so said goodbye to Todd and good morning to Donna. She asked how my night went and if I had heard anything yet. This was a question most would ask every day. I walked to my room and stood looking out the window at the rain falling softly watching the birds gather something to eat.

I heard, 'Good morning, Lucinda' and turned to face Dr Hartman coming to work. He said he was going to look over the lab reports from a few days ago and then be down to talk with me before his appointments. I had breakfast and was braiding my hair when he came in. He had me sit on the bed and he sat at the foot pulling over the bed table while looking at the clipboard his news I did not like.

'Lucinda', he said. 'I don't like the results of the last tests for I am concerned that there are too many parasites not being destroyed by the treatments and I don't want them to attack your organs, which could already be happening". He explained that there had been studies showing that Chemotherapy was used for some forms of tropical blood disorders. He asked me if I was ready to try it for he felt we had to look at this to save my life. Of course I put him in God's hands and told him exactly that. Covering my face with my hands and sighing great big for I didn't want to cry, he came over and kissed the top of my head. He told me he wanted to get started right away so was going to have Donna come in and help him. He explained that I would get a treatment every week for possibly 6 weeks but he would be monitoring my blood each week to see if it was I needed.

He and Donna were back and he told me I would possibly not feel good and to let Donna know every symptom I was experiencing. I promised as they got to work on me. Within an hour I was feeling upset in my tummy and tried to go to sleep.

I did fall asleep and when I woke I was not feeling too bad but laid still and tried to watch TV to keep my mind busy. I got my journal out and was writing in it when Donna came in with Nancy. She asked if I felt like some soup and I said I would try it. It was just broth so handled it quite well. Later I got out of bed and put my robe on and walked a little in the hall. Just as I walked toward the nurse's station I heard Dr Hartman's voice and he was asking Nancy how I was doing. I said, 'I am doing fine' and he turned with this big smile and said, 'So you are'! He said goodnight and reminded Nancy to call if she needed him. He walked over and patted me on the head and walked down the hall to the back door by my room. He called back and told me to keep drinking lots of water and said I was doing a great job on walking, as he opened the door and went out.

The next week went fine and I kept checking my hair to see if it was all attached and it was. Nancy had mentioned one evening that I might loose some but probably not in the early stages. My hair was quite long and I really thought I should go to the Base Exchange beauty shop and have it cut below my shoulders. Maybe if I start loosing it I will have them just shave me and get someone to take my hair and make me a wig. Need to ask Heather if she thinks I should do it and if so who she would suggest.

Today is the second round so I was very nervous waiting on Dr. Hartman to come and tell me what the lab test showed yesterday. Donna came in with breakfast and while I was eating in came my doctor and I watched his face as he walked across the room to my bed. He sat down studying the clipboard and I think I had not taken a breath until he told me it looked good but he still wanted me to have another injection. Of course I said fine and once again he came over and this time kissed the top of my head and walked out. Donna came in to get my tray and said they would be back but wanted my breakfast to settle and this time they would be giving me something to help me with the nausea. Thanking her I leaned back and waited for them to come.

When they finished he reminded me again to drink plenty of water and if I get too dehydrated they would give me an IV. I told them as long as I knew to do it I would. 'Try getting more exercise and keep writing in your journal,' he remarked. Donna asked me if I liked jigsaw puzzles and I told her I did so she brought me one.

I made it through the day with only a slight upset tummy but didn't want any lunch. I said to Donna, 'Maybe some toast without butter later'. I got up and walked to the window as the birds were now climbing on the sill as if to talk to me. When I went out I would put crumbs up on the sill to make them not be afraid of me. I wanted to take some toast out later when they brought me some and feed them again.

Time had gotten away from me for I was getting brain fog and couldn't concentrate on writing in my journal. Dr Hartman told me not to beat myself up if I couldn't finish a sentence or work on my puzzles. 'Just work on them a few minutes and quit. You can go back to them later', he would remind me. 'Just build up to when you're feeling comfortable, it's like your muscles, sometimes you have to train your mind to work harder. I certainly didn't like not being in control of my thoughts and I would cry often. I would tell myself to concentrate and then reminding myself of what the good doctor said about progress comes with time.

# Chapter 15

## No, Not My Hair

By the fourth week of chemo I could not keep anything on my tummy so I was drinking and taking nourishment from the IV's. I had started loosing my hair so Heather had one of the girls from the base exchange come and shave my head and saving my 'locks' to make me a wig. I cried myself to sleep after she left. Heather had bought me a cute head scarf with pink flowers and one was yellow paisley print that had a band and small bill on the front. I didn't want anyone to see me or say anything to me so I just covered up and tried to sleep the hurt away. In the middle of the night I woke up and found my doctor lying in a chair with his feet propped up on the foot of my bed. He had gotten a pillow and blanket and was sound asleep. I crawled down and laid my head close to his feet putting my hand on his leg and feel back to sleep. When I woke up the blanket was back on me and he was gone.

It wasn't a good morning for I hurt all over again and just couldn't move to get out of bed. I knew I should walk around as usual but I could not even straighten up this morning. I climbed back in bed and was crying to the Lord to help me regain my strength. I wanted to go out to the courtyard but afraid to try it without help. I buzzed for Donna and she came in all cheery, as usual, but when I looked up at her I started crying, for she had shaved her head too. We hugged and she reminded me that I was not only a patient of hers but she had learned to really care as a friend for me and said, 'This is what friends do for one another.' We hugged and cried together. What a great group of lovely people God has brought into my life. I told her I could not get through this stuff if it wasn't for all the caring people that the Lord gave me.

I then asked her if I could shower and she said to wait until she finished a couple of jobs and she would come back in and help me. As she was helping me out of the shower I asked her if Dr Hartman was in yet and she said she hadn't seen him. I wanted so bad to get dressed and walk around so she helped me put a spirit of hope in me. I wanted to put on a clean pair of surgery clothes. We laughed as she reminded me it doesn't take long anymore for you in the shower with no long hair to wash and then laughed and said, 'me either'. I thought I would normally cry but this morning I laughed! Thank you Lord.

I climbed back on the bed and tried to do some stretches and turns as Dr Hartman came in. We just stared at each other and he said, 'bald people are cuter and live longer and rubbed my head with a kiss. Laughing he said, 'Donna even looks younger'! We laughed and then I thanked him for watching over me last night. I told him he didn't need to do that but he needed to be home with his family. Looking at me he didn't say anything for a while and I thought he was studying my chart. He looked up at me and said I don't have a family to go home to. I was shocked and embarrassed and then he said his wife had left him five years ago and his son, Bret, was in college in Oregon and living with his grandparents. He looked at me and I told him I was so sorry but he reassured me it was fine. He offered that his wife didn't want him to join the reserves but hoped they would settle in Oregon. When he got Hickam she was fine but didn't like flying back and forth to see her family and friends. 'The last time she went she never came back', he said. 'I raised my boy and he wanted to go into medicine so moved to Oregon.' He got up and said he had appointments but would be back later.

Before he left for his appointments he said there would not be any need for the sixth treatment for they thought it had killed most of the parasites and if they do anything it will be a blood transfusion and see how many come to the new blood source. He said we will be waiting on them with antibiotics and I think this will take care of the active ones.

As he walked to the door he turned and asked me, rubbing his bald head, if I wanted to borrow any of his 'head gel' and he would even show me how to put it on. I laughed and said, 'maybe if it needed it he could show me how'.

As the weeks turned into months I was enjoying now getting out and attending church with the Conner's and even Dr Hartman once in a while would come by and get me. I am looking so forward in getting the last of my transfusions this month. Dr Hartman is hoping that if there are any parasites left they would leave my organs and come and get the 'fresh stuff'. He will start me on antibiotics if they show up.

General Bradley called and asked if Brad had called and I told him he had not. I was to call him back by the end of the day and let him know for he would make one more phone call to Brad's commander and then take matters into his own hands. I thank God for these caring people who have taken me under their wings.

The Lord answered my prayer that morning for I got the call that I had been waiting on. As I picked up the phone all I heard was crying for I knew it had to be Bonnie. Of course I started crying too. I thought she would have been in school so asked her if there was no school today. She, crying, told me Brad had told her last night and she couldn't sleep so didn't go. Then I heard the words that really made me cry, she hated her new step-mom and spent most of her time at her friend's house. She said they were always flying to Vegas and left her alone but she wasn't allowed to leave the house. I wanted so bad to tell her to come but of courseI had no place for her. Telling her to hang in there for I could possibly be out in a month or two and then it would be Thanksgiving break for her. Trying to get her hopes up a little I told her that they were trying to find me a place to stay on base for I would have to come in every 3-4 weeks for blood tests and they knew I did not have money to rent a place. She said she was ready to come even though she hated to leave her friends. We talked about her sisters and found out when they got married and to whom. She said they were doing fine and that Brad's new wife was given them money to help them out. They gave Donny and his wife money for a home. I was so happy to hear that their dad was making up for his time away from them and now he could help them in some way. When she told me that Becky had married a military man and was now she has found out she is pregnant with their first baby. Also that Donny was still going to school and his new wife had only a part time job. I could not hold back the tears and cried so hard that I told Bonnie I would have to call her back if that was alright. She cried with me and said I would have to call in the mornings before she went to school for her dad did not want her to call me. He just allowed her this one call.

After hanging up I could not control my hurt and remembered Donna coming in rubbing my back as I lay there crying. I must have fallen to sleep for when I woke Donna had left but Dr Hartman was sitting in the chair looking out the window. I got up and he came over to me and asked me if there was anything he could do or if I wanted to talk. I asked him to call General Bradley and tell him Bonnie had called and then I started to cry again. He sat near me and put his arms around me and just held me as I cried. I kept saying I was sorry and he just kept saying, 'get it out for I know you are hurting'. He got up and said, 'Let's go for a walk, you haven't been out and it is a beautiful evening'. While I got on my walking shoes he called General Bradley to tell him Bonnie had to wait possibly until Thanksgiving to come.

How did I ever deserve such caring people? He let me do most of the talking and whenever I would stop and control a sob he would take my hand. Finally he never let it go and I felt so moved and wondered why my heart was beating faster. Could it be that I was getting out of breath from walking. Or?????

# Chapter 16

# The Return of Hair

Time has really flown by; it was almost time for Bonnie to be here . . . . One more month!! I have finished all the treatments so now it was time for the blood transfusions again to build up my immune system. I pray for no more parasites to be in the blood or organs. Every morning as I dry off from my shower I can see the hair is growing more and more. As Donna's hair is coming in fast, mine is not so quick. She is looking good!

Dr Hartman is stopping once in awhile in the evenings to go walking with me. I keep telling him he doesn't have to do that for I know he probably would rather run. He mentioned that when he drops me off he runs home and that is just enough for him. He seemed to care and he said he liked getting to know me.

Donna had brought me a radio so it was wonderful to sit in the window and listen to a Christian music station. I would sing along and loved getting my voice back and especially my breathing as my lungs taken a beating from the chemo. Walking has really helped me there. I even think the birds liked the music. They were beginning to sit on the outside sill even while I sat there. Today my voice was joyful and as I was singing I heard a voice singing along with me and turned to see Dr Hartman coming toward me smiling. I got very embarrassed but managed to tell him he had a wonderful voice. He just looked at my feet and said, 'Are you ready to go walking'? I thought to myself, but it was not our day.

I got my shoes on and went out the door and saw Dr Hartman driving off so thought he was probably going home. As I got to the top of the hill near the park where the officers housing area is and where the Connors and Dr Hartman lives, he was running up the hill toward me.

He stopped and turned around to walk with me and ask me, 'Do you like playing card games?' I responded, 'I sure do!' 'Well, I'll bring over some tonight, if you're not busy?' he asked. I laughed and said, 'Oh, I think my calendar is free tonight'. We both laughed and he took off running yelling back not to eat supper in the cafeteria. I turned around and headed back to the hospital for a good shower would feel wonderful. I took extra work on my make-up but not over doing it so he would not see much difference in my appearance. It didn't take too much time as I didn't have my hair to worry about. Putting on one of my flowered lounge dresses, I hoped I was not going to put more into this dinner than I should.

Gee, I was really excited about getting together with Dr Hartman and wondering what he was bringing for supper tonight. I really didn't know how to set my room up for playing games so asked Terri in the cafeteria if I could borrow a table and two chairs. I told her Dr Hartman was bringing in my supper so she even gave me a table cloth. How sweet of her! I set them up under the big window that looked out over the courtyard. I went down to the nurse's station and asked Nancy if she had a candle or something I could burn in my room. She looked in the cabinets and low and behold she found a nice Vanilla scented one and also handed me some matches. I told her my room smelt like a hospital room! We both laughed and she went off to check a light that was blinking from a patient's room. I went back to my room to light the candle, put it on the table and shut the door so the room would smell better faster. I turned on the radio to a station with mellow type music and then I started pacing back and forth looking out the window. Why did I feel nervous? It was like a date and I wanted it to be just right. Although I don't want to get my hopes built up for he was the commander of the hospital and maybe I shouldn't feel this way.

As I was smoothing my bedding to make it look neater I heard a gasping sound, 'Wow, I think you were expecting someone! 'Was this for me?' I turned around with a little embarrassed feeling like I had over done it and said, 'My doctor is bringing dinner so I wanted to show him how much I appreciated his thoughtfulness'. I continued and walked to the table saying, 'Do you think he would like it?' He came over and laid down a take-out bag with one hand and from behind him he pulled out a bouquet of flowers. I started crying, saying, 'Thank you, thank you, they are beautiful!' I pulled out a large glass from under my bedside stand and went to put water in it while Dr Hartman set the table. The food smelled like Japanese or Chinese food and I loved it. I put the flowers on the table and remarked, 'What a beautiful center piece for our table!' He had thought of everything, from silverware to napkins and glasses for WINE that he had brought. I quickly asked, 'Can I have wine?' He looked at me and reminded me that he was the doctor and of course I could. Embarrassed I said, 'Yes, I forgot for a moment.' He then came over as I was just about to pull my chair out and he grabbed it for me to sit down. Then he sat and took my hand to offer grace for our food, but kept holding it and our eyes locked and I think he saw that I was breathing hard so let go. Oh, my gosh! My heart was out of control!

As I took a drink of the cool water I regained my regular heart beat and Dr Hartman poured a glass of wine and held it up for a toast. I started shaking again as he smiled and said, 'To many more relaxed evenings'. That was it! Of course I responded, 'Yes'.

While we ate he told me he was going to have to go to the states for temporary duty to a base in California as one of the surgeons there had a heart attack. They needed him to fill in while they searched for someone to come in permanently. He said it looks like about six weeks! He stared at my reaction and I guess I gave one that he seemed to like for he just smiled and stared. My eyes watered up and I said, 'Who will take your place here?' He answered, "Dr Conner's knows your case as I consult with him all the time'. He told me he was leaving the next day and I looked down at my plate and thinking to myself that I shouldn't show my feelings.

That evening was so great and he made me laugh so much that I forgot about him leaving in the morning. Finally he reminded me that he would have to go home and pack. He picked up his dishes that he brought and I walked him to the outside door where he had parked his car. I thanked him for a wonderful thoughtful evening and added that I would be praying for him in the new surroundings. He turned around and pulled me by my waist toward him and kissed me! Then I felt my arms go around his shoulders and kissed him back. He then kissed my forehead and walked to his car.

I turned on the radio and there was a station that played the 50's and 60's type music. I turned out the lights and left on the bed light and was just dancing around the room. I thought if I could just exercise and dance maybe I would sleep. It was getting late and I was wearing out so was just swaying around the room and doing slow moves with my eyes closed when I felt arms around my waist. I looked around to find it was Dr Hartman. He kissed my neck and we just swayed until the song stopped. He turned to go and said he had forgot some paper work so came back and saw me so couldn't resist holding me one more time. He pulled my head down and kissed the top of my head while tears started forming. I would be able to go to sleep tonight that is for sure. I did sleep off and on but for some reason when I got out of bed this morning I did not feel tired.

Donna had just arrived and saw my flowers and questioned me of who the giver was. When I told her it was Dr Hartman she looked and said, 'He did not want to leave right now for he felt he was letting you down.' She saw my reluctance to answer and reminded me that Dr Conner's would be in touch with Dr Hartman all the way. I smiled and agreed that he was also a very caring doctor. Donna went on to say that Dr Hartman had put in an order for more blood work since it had been a while. 'No breakfast, till after they take your blood', she said. I remarked that it was all going to be good for I was feeling great. I put on my walking shoes to go out this morning before they came to take my blood. I reported to the nurse's station that I would be back and Donna gave me the 'Atta-girl' thumbs up and see me when I get back.

I don't know why I walked a different path this morning but walked down into the housing area where Dr Hartman and Heather lived. As I was going by Heather's house she was coming out the front door with her dog Honey and she was taking her for a walk. What a fun walk and I really got to know more about her. She told me that Guy had been over to their house the night before and seemed down because he had to leave. Then a question that I was not expecting, 'What are your feelings for Guy?' She continued, 'He told us what he was going to do last night and we were both getting excited that he has not shown any feelings for any woman for several years'. We sat on the park bench to let Honey run and there was silence as I wasn't sure how much I should tell her about my feelings. I started off by saying, 'I think he is a wonderful doctor and sometimes I do think of him more than being my doctor'. I continued, 'Especially after last night'. I didn't tell her he had kissed me as he left. She told me that he had asked Perry if it was 'talk' amongst the hospital staff about him and me. They felt Guy was a very caring doctor but noticed he did spend a lot more time with my case and in my room. Since I was one of only three patients that he was in charge of Perry thought he was devoting his time equally. Heather said that people had commented about him picking me up to take me to church, walking with me and coming to my room at night to play cards. Guy didn't want to be transferred because of this so wanted his 'friends' advice. I asked her,

'Do you think that is why they sent him to the base in California?' She remarked, 'Possibly'.

I had to remind myself that Donna was waiting on me so left her with Honey playing and hugged her for sharing with me. She said, 'We both think a lot of you and Guy so we will pray for God's Will and watch Him direct you both to see where your relationship goes'. I thanked her and off I went.

Walking in the back door I saw Donna peeking around the corner and said, 'Get your shower for the lab is on their way'. Knowing it would not take me long I was out before they got there and in my bed waiting.

Knowing I would not hear today about the blood work I still was apprehensive of the results. Praying for the Lord's will I felt peace and napped as I hadn't slept too well last night. It was a good 'lack-of-sleep' feeling as I pondered over that special time. As I was day dreaming my phone ran and it was Dr Hartman telling me he got there and gave me his number if I needed to call. He said, 'For any reason'. I knew he meant it and again thanked him for a wonderful evening. My heart gave a leap as he said, 'My pleasure and I look forward to many more'. Of course I responded back, 'Me too as it has been the high-light of my stay there'. He told me when he walked in my room and saw what I had done he knew I was having feelings too. He went on to say that maybe the Lord wanted us to think about this and that is why He was sent to the states for a spell. He asked if I had the blood work done and I told him I did so he felt he would know something in the morning and Dr Conner's would let me know. He also said he would call me tomorrow night and talk to me about it. He said he had to go and would be praying for the results to be great.

The next morning I got up and showered and was waiting on Donna to come in to let me know if I could go down and get some breakfast. She said the reports had not come in yet so to wait. I decided to catch up on my writing in my journal for I wanted to put my feelings down while they were still fresh from my 'date-night' with Dr Hartman. I knew I would have to continue to call him doctor as it may be a red flag to others. If Heather was right many of the staff already knows but I don't want to hurt his career in any way or make him get permanent orders away from here. Just then Dr Conner's came in breaking my thoughts for my journal. I closed it up and told him to sit down, pointing to the foot of the bed. That is where Dr Hartman liked to sit. He said, 'Good morning Lucinda'. I responded, 'Good morning to you too'. He went on to say, 'I heard you had a great night last night?' I looked at him for a moment to try and figure out what he wanted me to say. I smiled and said, 'It was a great night until Dr Hartman told me he had to go stateside'. Then I added, 'Not because you are taking over my case for I know you and Dr Hartman talk all the time and I trust you too'. He thanked me and then what he said next made me gasp for I was so sure I wouldn't hear those words again. 'Lucinda, we're uneasy about the results of the blood work and we aren't sure yet which antibiotic we should use. We don't want to go chemo yet. By then I was crying and saying, 'No, No, No, I have been feeling good'. Just as I got those words out Heather walked in and came over and sat holding me just letting me cry it out. I knew Dr. Conner had called her with the results and felt Heather was second best to Dr Hartman! I heard Dr. Conner say he would be back later. Just then the phone rang and Heather went around to answer it was Guy. She said, 'I am going to see Perry and be back'. When I said hello to Dr Hartman he was so sorry that he wasn't there to have been the one to tell me. Then he said, 'Do you want me to fly back for the week-end?' I started crying again but told him no. He needed to be there and I felt God was in control and would get me through it again. He said he would call me tonight and hung up.

# Chapter 17

# Bonnie for Thanksgiving

When Dr. Conner came into my room he told me that Dr Hartman was afraid that if we didn't do the strong dose of antibiotics the parasites that were just born might get into my organs. I wanted so much to be well by Thanksgiving for Bonnie was talking about maybe coming and Heather already had told me she could stay with them for that time. Now I don't know what to do but all I knew was I wanted to see her and I needed her while I went through this treatment. Heather said to pray about it for she knew I wouldn't want Bonnie to worry about me. I was thankful it was not chemo for now anyway. I waited until 2am to call Bonnie and told her but she insisted she wanted to be here. Now if I can just wait the three weeks until she arrives!

Donna came in with Dr. Conner and the tech people to start my antibiotic IV. Dr. Conner stated that Dr. Hartman thought a strong dose would be all I would need so already I was praising the Lord. Dr Conner turned to me and said, 'Well, one thing for sure is that you don't have to worry about losing anymore hair.' I was so grateful for that comment as it was coming in so good now. I turned the radio on to keep my mind on singing praise songs and wanting the Lord to know I was trusting him all the way and had faith that I would not be as sick. Getting out my journal again to catch up on the days activities I tried to be optimistic about it all and thought if the girls were to read my journal some day they would know I counted on the Lord, more and more each day. From the day of the crash I felt God had something special planned for me and I was trying to keep it in His hands.

As three weeks had now gone by, it was time for another blood test. I was anxious this morning to see how clean my blood would be with all the antibiotics that had been pumped in me the last couple of weeks. I was eager to call Bonnie in the AM hours to see how she was doing on the flight. General Bradley had arranged her flight and Dr Hartman was going to meet her at the base terminal to make sure she got off without hitches. Brad had put her on the base shuttle bus from where he was and it would take her about 4 hours to get here. Dr. Hartman wanted to make sure she wasn't going to be afraid. When he had called me to tell me what he was going to do, I felt he was the most caring man I knew. He even offered his home but Heather said she was looking forward to having her there.

Heather knew I would be antsy so came and got me to go to her house and see how she had fixed up Bonnie's room. It was so precious and even had books for her to read. She was asking me what all she like to eat and I told her I was sure her taste had changed in three years so would have to wait until she arrived to ask. I would have her eat with me in the cafeteria at first. When she was young she was a little particular about how foods were prepared. We sat and drank some hot tea and talked about Bonnie for I had not really shared a lot about her. She seemed just as nervous as I to see her tomorrow. It would be in the late afternoon but Dr Hartman said he would call as soon as she was on the plane. Then to wait another 5 hours was going to be so hard. She invited me for lunch and then we waited for Dr Connor to come home. Dr Connor drove me back to the hospital for I knew I must get my journal all caught up for I was not going to have a lot of time while Bonnie was here. Going to bed early was a welcome thought for I had not taken a nap today.

I woke up to the birds chirping outside my window. It was like they knew it was going to be a beautiful day for me and for them as well. Coming back from the cafeteria I heard my phone ringing, so I quickly got to it before it quite and found it was my adorable doctor telling me he had just put Bonnie on the plane. He went on to tell me she hugged him and thanked him for taking such good care of her mother all this time. He said, 'I told her I think your mother is a very special lady and for that matter so does the whole hospital staff'. He continued, 'She hugged me crying and saying she hoped she would see me again.' I told her, 'There was never a doubt, and that he would be home soon.' By now I was crying while telling him, 'Thank you for everything'. Then he said, 'I plan on collecting when I get back.' My heart starting racing again as I knew this man was for me.

I called Heather to tell her and she sounded just as excited. I told her I was going to lie down and hopefully fall asleep for a couple of hours. She said the terminal told her they would call when the plane was in bound. I could then start walking toward her house and she would pick me up on the way.

I managed to take that nap and felt great when I woke up. Three hours to wait! I knew Bonnie and I had so much to catch up on and I wanted to know exactly what happened the last three years that I missed out on. I went down to the front desk to see if I could help the aids pass out magazines to pass the time. They gave me a cart for my floor so I could stay near the phone. Job done and Bonnie was due in about 30 minutes. As I was walking in my room the phone rang and I was so nervous I about dropped it. It was Heather so I took off out the door and ran to where I saw her driving up the street.

We walked into the terminal just as the plane was landing. Tears started rolling down my face and Heather grabbed my hand. We then saw Bonnie walking toward the building and a tall airman carrying one suitcase and her the other. I ran to the window and was crying and waving. She was crying too but I couldn't get near her until she had cleared the processing of her arrival. Then we grabbed each other and just let all the tears flow. Heather came over and put her arms around us both crying. All of a sudden flashes went off and we turned to see people taking pictures. They came over and asked us how it felt to be together again after all these years. I hurriedly put my arms around Bonnie and walked her out to the car. I asked Heather how they knew about us and she was just as shocked as I was. I remember when I first got to Hickam a television station reporter had come by to ask me questions but Dr Hartman had handled that so hadn't seen anyone since.

I sat in the back seat with Bonnie so I could just keep hugging her. She was so pretty and had grown up more than I had imagined that she had. She was wearing glasses now and had pretty long dark hair.

Heather took Bonnie to her room and put her luggage on the floor telling her she could unpack at her leisure. She left us in the bedroom and I asked Bonnie if she was hungry and tired. She said she was both but we could talk if I wanted to. I quickly called Dr Hartman to tell him Bonnie had arrived and thanked him again for taking care of her so sweetly. He was ready for bed so we said good night.

Dr Connor was due home and Heather said she wanted me to stay and have dinner with them too. We went out to help set the table and in walked Dr Conner. Right away he came over to Bonnie as I introduced her to him and he gave her a big hug. She hugged him back and told him she was so thankful for helping me get better. Of course Dr Hartman's name was mentioned!! After dinner we did the dishes and sat in the living room talking. I turned to Bonnie and asked if I could help her unpack and she said she would do it in the morning as she just wanted to go to bed. I knew this was mentally draining on her and I just couldn't imagine all the thoughts that were going through her precious mind right now. She took a shower and came out to say good night so I followed her in as she climbed in bed she started crying and asked me to stay till she fell asleep. Of course I would! We held each other and believe it or not both of us fell asleep until I felt a tapping on my arm to find Heather. I quietly got up and went out to the living room. I told her Bonnie had wanted me to lay down with her until she fell asleep. Heather said it was late so took me back to the hospital. I was so tired but a happy tired and went right to sleep.

The phone woke me up and it was Dr Hartman checking to see how things were and how I was feeling. I told him I had wished he could have been there to share my happiness. He said, 'I knew you two would be off somewhere today so wanted to check in early. He told me the good news that the blood work that was taken did not show any signs of new parasites. I was still anemic. He wanted to get that taking care of first so ordered a different diet for me to follow. He said that Dr Conner would get with the nutritionist and have the cafeteria start it today. He then told me that he was going to Oregon to have Thanksgiving with his son and parents. Knowing that I would be wrapped up with Bonnie here he thought maybe he could get back for Christmas. I told him Bonnie wasn't going back until Tuesday so we had 4 days to talk and have fun together. I asked him when he would be back to the base and he said he was only staying until Sunday but would be happy to meet Bonnie and get her on the shuttle going home. I thanked him and he said he had a plane to catch so wished me a Happy Thanksgiving and he would see me in a few weeks. Weeks sounded so much better than saying a month for I really did miss him. He added that if Bonnie and I wanted some private time that we could go to his house.

I got my shower and ate breakfast before walking down to Heathers. I didn't want Bonnie having to drag all her photo albums or yearbooks to the hospital. Heather said I was welcome to come there to be with Bonnie. I liked the idea that Dr Hartman mentioned and would ask Bonnie if she wanted to do that for I wanted to know about her step mom. When I got to the house, Heather said, 'Bonnie is still asleep'. I remember that she always liked to sleep in on Saturday mornings and it was very hard to get her up on school days. I thought I would let her sleep until 9 and then wake her for we only had four days.

As Heather and I were drinking some tea in the kitchen Bonnie walked out. She was hungry so ate a bowl of cereal and listened to us talk. I told Heather that Dr Hartman had called and offered his house if Bonnie and I wanted some private time. She thought that was so sweet of him and then left for the commissary to get things for our Thanksgiving dinner tomorrow. I offered to make the pumpkin pie so she said, 'There is lunch meat for sandwiches when we get hungry and that Perry was eating at the hospital today. I told her I could do that while she was gone. Getting out all the ingredients I started making the pastry while Bonnie started showing me the album pictures of Donny and Becky's wedding. Asking her why they wanted to get married so soon she told me that Donny and his wife, Candy, had dated for 2 years and as soon as he graduated they got married. He got a full scholarship at UCLA and wanted to go on to college. Bonnie said Candy was helping at a day-care when she was not in school and was promised full time this year. That helped toward their finances but until then Brad's new wife was giving them money. Bonnie said that Brad met her in Las Vegas and her dad owned several casinos and had lots of money. She told me that she would hear her dad and wife arguing a lot and it seemed her daddy didn't want her marrying Brad. Bonnie was so tired of hearing them fight about money all the time then she would go back to daddy and Brad would go get her. I reminded her she needed to keep praying for them and I was sure the Lord would give her peace about their relationship.

I told her I was getting close to getting out of the hospital and that the General was keeping an ear out for a place, like a guest house, for me to temporary live in while I was an out-patient. She would be a junior and felt if she came this summer it wouldn't be hard to leave but waiting until she was a senior she would want to graduate with her friends. Her best friend's parents got orders for the other base here in Hawaii so she knew she would not mind coming.

By this time, the cut up bread for the dressing and pie were in the oven. I had now seen all of the wedding pictures and family ones that Bonnie had brought. She was ready to start on the yearbooks so I started getting the pastry ready for the pecan pie that Heather said she wanted to do. She was going to do that for she had a special filling.

The pie, sandwiches, bread for dressing cut up was done and also another yearbook looked at when Heather walked in. The phone rang and Dr Hartman was at the airport and wanted to tell me where the key was for the front door. To myself I thought, 'I think he is missing us'! I know I am him but didn't say it out loud.

Heather came home a couple of hours later so we helped her carry in the groceries and she was pleased that I had accomplished so much. I told her you can do a lot when you're listening to someone talk. She was glad to hear Bonnie was telling me so much. We sat down and had a sandwich before we started organizing the rest of tomorrow's dinner. I told Heather that Bonnie and I were going to walk down to the hospital and take her the walking route so she could walk up in the mornings if she would like. Also I mentioned that Dr Hartman had called to tell us where the key was and that if I wanted to stay over at night with Bonnie we could sleep in his king sized bed. I was thinking we might do that the last night she was here. She thought that was so sweet of him and didn't blame us. I had never been in his house so was a little curious to what I might find!

We walked down to the hospital and Bonnie thought all the staff at the hospital was so nice. She was happy to see how they could be like a family. I went down to ask Dr Conner if he would come by and take Bonnie back to his house when he got off work. He said he would be happy to and it would probably be in about 30 minutes. We went back to my room and waited. I could tell she was getting tired as the time change made it bed time for her. I told her I would walk down in the morning to help Heather with dinner. Dr Conner and Bonnie went home. I must admit I was tired too. Much had been done, all the conversation talk and trying to put it all together, about all she told me. I took another shower to relax me and set down to watch some TV.

Nancy woke me up with an IV set-up and said Dr Hartman felt I needed to start getting some iron supplements by fluid in me. She laid some papers on my table and said you can read these to see what all you will be required to do by the Nutritionist. 'Nancy, why couldn't this have waited until Friday?' I said, she answered, 'Dr Hartman knew you would be tied up with your daughter so wanted it done at night while you sleep'. 'Oh, that is a wise and thoughtful idea'. I said. Then she commented that Dr Hartman is always thinking about you and walked out of my room. Now this made me uneasy for this is what I had questioned Heather about and hoped it was not hurting Dr Hartman if he was paying more attention to me than others. I must ask Dr Connor in private tomorrow about that comment from Nancy. I turned out the lights and slipped in bed not even watching TV.

I woke up a couple of times as my IV was sticking and hurting, but all in all I slept very well. I looked down and the IV was gone so I must have slept through it being taken out. I was anxious to get down to see Bonnie so I showered and got dressed. Cafeteria was closed as it was a holiday! All the patients were released and I was the only one there. Dr Conner knew I would be at their house so he let all the staff off except the ER staff.

I knew Dr Conner and Heather would be up by 8 so walked down. Bonnie was still asleep so I was able to talk to Dr Conner about Nancy's remark. Heather was putting the turkey in the oven. He assured me that what people were saying was not damaging to Dr Hartman for most of the people saw a big change in him and liked it. He went on to say that I had made an impression on everyone there and was well liked. He reassured me that they liked the idea of Dr Hartman maybe being interested in me. He commented that even General Bradley was doing things that were out of the usual. Tears came and he patted me on the hand and said that he and Heather had noticed. This was only because of their friendship and knowing Guy was a very sincere man for he would never do anything to jeopardize his career. He has too many people who think the world of him and would vouch for his conduct any day of the week. As far as what Heather and I think, Guy wants to be involved with you more but wants to wait until you are out of the hospital. My heart wanted to skip right out of my chest with happiness but I was still trying to control my feelings in front of Dr Conner. I know that Heather has told him how I feel about Dr Hartman but I too didn't want to hurt his career. I told Dr Conner that I thought it was all in God's plan for him to leave for a spell while I get better and the chances of leaving the hospital would be greater by the time he was due back. He agreed and would help that happen by getting me dismissed.

Bonnie woke up and was coming into the kitchen just as we finished our talk. I was thankful that she didn't know yet of my feelings for my doctor.

She came over and hugged me saying, 'good morning'. I went out to see what I could do to help Heather. She had baked some cinnamon rolls and was putting them on a plate. We all sat down at the table; Bonnie with hot chocolate and the rest of us with coffee or tea. Thanking the Lord for the day and what it means was our conversation over our breakfast. I truly had to win the most powerful blessing for this year! While eating the phone rang, it was Dr Hartman wishing all of us a Happy Thanksgiving. They had just got up from the table with full tummies. Bonnie remarked that he sure was a caring doctor but remembered he lived across the street and was the Conner best friend.

Friday morning Heather took the day off and we went over to Bellows Air Station at the beach. It was so beautiful and not any people on the beach. We watched a couple of sail boats that were decorated for it looked like a boat with a film crew. We had packed a picnic lunch of turkey sandwiches and had a great day of swimming and walking on the beach. Bonnie fell in love with Hawaii and couldn't wait until she could come to stay. We talked about the timing as I needed to find a job and place before she could come. I told her and Heather I was going to start looking in the paper to see what was being offered. It was getting late and I knew sitting under the beach umbrella had brought had not kept us from getting sun burned. We, however, did plaster the sun screen on us several times. Bonnie said, 'Well, I guess the film crew didn't want to put us in the movie so we might as well leave. We laughed and started packing up our belongings.

As soon as we walked in the house the phone was ringing and it was Dr Hartman asking us how our day went. Again Bonnie remarked that he sure was calling a lot. She asked Heather if he was interested in momma or what? Heather looked at me and said, 'That question you will have to ask your mom'. Of course that was our topic when we were alone. Just telling her that we did have feelings for each other but it was only very good friends. I did not want to hurt his career. She thought it was great for she liked him. I told her that he going to work at the base in California. It gave me time to find a place and be released from the hospital. Even then I didn't know when he would be back. She asked if we could stay at his house for the next two nights and talk about her coming. I told Heather what she wanted to do and she was glad we were getting some alone time.

Bonnie and I talked most of the night and I wanted to know if she was still involved in the youth group at the chapel on base. She said she was because this got her away from the house more. I was so glad that she was open to talk about what she was doing and so happy to hear she was still attending church, even telling me about her feelings in living with her dad and new step-mom. I was sorry that the arrangement couldn't be better but if it had been, she wouldn't be thinking of coming to live with me. All the more was the urgency to get a job.

Saturday was here and we walked down to the Base Exchange for Bonnie to see if there was anything she wanted. I had kept some money out just for her trip. She wanted me to save it while I looked for a job. I couldn't wait to take her to church with me tomorrow so she would get to meet the rest of my friends. I picked up our supper and we walked back home to Dr Hartman's house. Heather was in the yard with Honey and we walked over to pet her. Bonnie had also taken a liking to her and Honey loved playing with Bonnie. She asked us if we wanted to come to dinner and I told her that Bonnie wanted pizza so we were going to watch a movie and eat pizza. As I was putting the pizza in the oven to keep it warm Dr Hartman called. I was not sure if I should answer it but Bonnie said, 'I'll bet it is the good doctor calling!' Sure enough he was getting ready for bed. He had an early flight back to the base and wanted to say goodbye to Bonnie. She took the phone and was very polite to him and then said, 'I hope you and my mom can see more of each other when you get back for I think you guys are good for each other'. She told him goodbye and thank you. I got on the phone and told him that statement was a complete surprise to me. He laughed and said, 'I'm glad she feels that way so now I have permission to pursue you.' I was silent for I had a tear rolling down my eye and Bonnie saw it. I said goodnight and she came over and hugged me. She said, 'Momma you deserve someone who cares that deeply for you'. I remarked back, 'Time will tell my sweet daughter'. We found a VHS movie to watch and ate pizza while laughing and crying but reminding ourselves we would soon be together each day.

General Bradley called and reminded us that Bonnie would have to be at the terminal by 9 on Tuesday morning. He would pick us up at 8 in case it took off early so she was on the list first. I knew we didn't have to worry with General Bradley handling it.

Before going to bed Bonnie started getting her suitcase packed and it was so hard to watch. That night we cuddled up together and I told her we needed to pray and ask the Lord to give her wisdom in helping her do the right thing. I was so proud that she had not forgot how to pray and ask forgiveness for anything that she had done and even about her dislike for her step-mom. God would help her understand and get along with both her dad and step mom. We then fell asleep.

Sunday and Monday were full of walking and talking and making plans for her to come back. I knew she couldn't come back for Christmas so we made plans for the summer school break. She wanted so much to come and stay but I told her this was going to have to be her decision and I would support it all the way.

Tuesday morning I woke up with the alarm going off so we each ran to a shower and got dressed. Just as we were putting our cereal bowls in the sink we heard the honk of the general. Bonnie picked up her suitcase and opened the door to General Bradley coming to the door and took the suitcase and put it in the back. He asked Bonnie about all she had done so I listened and could hear the excitement of her wanting to come back. General Bradley reached over and patted my hand and said I think I have a place for you. On the way back we will run by and look at it. I was so overwhelmed with gratitude tears were forming. I said, 'now to find a job, so could we pick up a paper on the way back?'

The terminal was full and I wondered if Bonnie would get bumped but when they called her name I was relieved that she would get home fine and Brad would not be mad. Crying, we said our goodbyes, I watched Bonnie walk to the plane. General Bradley came over and put his hand on my shoulder and said, 'She is coming back for sure'. I said, 'Yes, I think so'. We left and on the way home he stopped at a gas station to pick up a paper for me. Then left for Bellows Air Station and drove up to what looked like some guest cottages. We had seen those when we had been here at the beach on Friday. He drove up to one that had construction stuff all over the patio. We got out and he unlocked the door to what looked like a remodeling job going on. It was just that! General Bradley said this would be for Bonnie and me as it had a smaller bedroom for her. How wonderful that we would have two bedrooms and be near this beautiful beach that Bonnie loved. He said the cottage would not be ready for a month to six weeks. It wasn't a priority for the base as they didn't have a lot of guests staying there since it was a small air station and nothing to offer visitors. I told him that would be fine for I needed to find a job. I told him to drop me back at Dr Hartman's for I needed to change the bedding and wash our dishes that we used. He commented that Dr Hartman was a great man and they all loved the way he cared for his patients and took his profession very seriously. I agreed and we said our goodbyes and I thanked him for all his help. I went in and cleaned his home for him. Left him a note saying how thankful we were to have had such a great alone time. I walked back to the hospital very tired and took a nap. I wanted to get up at 2 AM and call Bonnie to see how her flight went.

## Chapter 18

# My First Interview

What a great night I had! I don't think I got up once. I looked at the clock and realized I had slept almost 12 hours. Oh, no! I wanted to call Bonnie! Now I will have to set my alarm tonight and wake up at 2am to call her. I told her I would.

After my shower and getting dressed I walked down to the nurse's station and Donna was doing paper work. She said she had come into my room several times but knew I must have had a very busy week-end with Bonnie so didn't wake me. She said I had only 15 minutes to get to the cafeteria for any breakfast and we would talk later.

As I was sitting at the table with my tea and newspaper Donna came in and said, 'So today is the day for job hunting, huh?' I told her all about Bonnie and our Thanksgiving time together. She was so pleased to hear that I would have her with me. I told her that she would have to make up her mind as to when she wanted to come. If her friend comes to Hawaii with her folks then I know she would come soon, next summer maybe. Sharing with her about the cottage guest house she was so excited for me. But now I need to find a job. She left my room and I started crossing out those I knew I needed a degree for and some that looked possible. My eye caught one that was looking for a live-in to care for a wheel-bound lady. It said spacious house and car available. How wonderful for I hadn't thought of a car and how in the world would I get to and from my job. Knowing I had the money I guess was not a concern for me. I circled it and wrote the information down on paper. As I looked on I really didn't see anything else that I felt I had experience in. Not that I had in caring for an elderly lady but wondered how hard it could be.

I had forgotten that I had not gone down to the chapel since Bonnie had been there and I really felt bad. I so wanted to let her know I was so dependent on the Lord for all my needs still. I made sure that the girls all went to church every Sunday. They were involved in youth and I even was teaching the 3-4th grade class. I really prayed that God would give me the wisdom to know what to do and put someone in my path that needed help. I liked people so knew that I could be a receptionist and learn clerical needs as I went. God had been so faithful to me and I knew he had the right work for me to do and I needed to wait on him to guide me to it.

Getting back to my room I decided to call this lady and when she answered the phone it was so sweet and cheery I thought to myself, 'I love this lady already'. When I told her who I was she got so excited and said she had told her caregiver lawyer that she wanted to help me. I asked her how she found out about me and she told me it was on the TV of my ordeal. I told her I had forgotten most of the conversation and I didn't remember much about the lady reporter coming by the hospital. I was so very weak and tired. She commented that she thought that I probably had been flown back to the states to be with my family. When she knew it was me she said she wanted to see me right away for they wanted to put her into a retirement center and she really didn't want to go. They had her interview several ladies but she did not feel comfortable with any of them. I said, 'Maybe the Lord was waiting on me to get well'. She started laughing and crying and asked, 'Honey, are you a child of God's'? I started crying too and said, 'You bet I am'. She told me her name was Margery and she wanted my phone number to call me after she talked to her lawyer. We hung up and I was so excited that I, ME, called Dr Hartman. Fortunately he was between meetings and when he heard my voice he asked, 'Are you alright?' I said, 'Yes, but I had to call you about this possible job I may be taking and what transpired!' I went on to ask, 'Is it alright if we talk?' He said, 'of course for I want to hear everything that you are doing'. As I told him of the conversation he talked like he was so thrilled and we both felt that God was guiding me to this woman. I told him she was going to call me back. He said he would call when he got back to his room.

I waited for two hours, had lunch, fed my birdies and walked a little in the hall outside my room. When the phone rang I knew it was her and she asked me if I could come and see her tomorrow. I told her that I was sure I could but would have to see if a nurse could bring me over. I asked what time and she said, 'how about lunch for both of you?' I said great but I would call her right back. I quickly went out to ask Donna if she could do it but she asked why I didn't call Heather. I told her I wanted her to assess Margery's condition. She said she would love to do it. I hugged her and thanked her. I called Margery right back and thanked her for seeing me on my nurses' lunch break. She said that her lawyer wanted to be there also and I said that would be great. It was around 3 pm and I figured Dr Hartman would be calling pretty soon so I didn't want to get far from the phone. I ran down to the cafeteria and got a bowl of soup and crackers and rushed back to my room.

While I was waiting Dr Conner's came in and wanted to tell me not to eat breakfast in the morning as it had been four weeks since my last blood test. He said he had heard about the cottage that General Bradley was getting ready for me but they were hoping I would be out in two weeks. I asked him if he had talked to the general about it and he said he had not. He left my room and the phone rang to find Dr Hartman on the other end. Of course he wanted to hear all about Bonnie's visit and what all we did. I was too excited about the interview with Margery I didn't tell him everything Bonnie and I did. I told him Dr Conner was just in and said I would be getting more blood tests tomorrow and that they wanted me to be dismissed in a couple of weeks. However, the general said the guest cottage wouldn't be ready for at least 6 weeks. Then I told him of my appointment tomorrow with Margery and maybe this is why the house isn't to be ready and I may be staying and caring for her. He was silent and then said, 'I will be happy with whatever you decide to do for I don't know how long I am to be assigned here. They are talking like they don't plan on finding a replacement and might wait until the other doctor can come back to work. I was silent then and he said, 'We will just have to keep praying for the Lord knows I want to be there with you and I hope you want to be with me.' I remarked that, 'You know that old saying that longing for each other will make the heart grow fonder'. 'Or something like that', I added. Then I said, 'I'll wait, no matter how long it takes'. He sweetly added, 'I wish I could be there to take you in my arms and know you really feel that way'. I said, 'Believe it'. He softly said, 'I do'. We talked for another hour and we said our goodnights and hung up. I turned on the TV for which I had not watched in a long time. Donna came in to say goodnight and see me in the morning. Behind her was Nancy and she took my vitals and said I was carrying a temperature. Donna heard her and came back into the room. She said to check me every couple of hours and if it didn't go up that the tests in the morning will help them find out what it is. I told her I was fine and had no aches but couldn't help wondering what it might be. Dr Conner came in on his way home and gave me a physical and said I should give Nancy a urine sample then he would have the results by morning. He said goodnight and out the door he went.

I was thankful that I didn't let this new news bother me from sleeping.

I woke up with the alarm going off and forgot that I had promised myself to call Bonnie. She was just going out the door but I told her of my interview with this lady about homecare and living with her. She was excited that I was finally getting out of the hospital but said she was meeting her friend at the end of the block so needed to go. We each said I love you and hung up.

The next thing I remember was the technician standing over me. I am sure he nudged me awake! Todd was with him as Nancy had left after her shift was over. When the tech left he took my temp and it was a degree higher than last night. It was about 6 and I knew Donna was to be at 7 so maybe the lab test for the urine sample were back and she would tell me something. I decided to get my shower and dressed to go for breakfast after Donna came in. I did not want to eat in case they needed more blood!

Finally about nine Donna came in and said they had three new patients from a serious car wreck so was busy helping them. She said Dr Conner was on his way for he had stopped by the lab to get my results. As she was turning to leave he walked in so she came back and stood beside me. He said the blood work was not done yet but the urine test showed I had a kidney infection or something going on with them. He had called Dr Hartman and he said to order a sonogram for this morning. I told him I had not eaten and he gave me thumbs up and left. Donna reassured me it would be done in time to go to my interview. I got undressed and put on one of the hospital gowns as she instructed me to do and wait. I had just gotten back to bed when they came in to wheel me down to x-ray. I prayed during my test for I wanted the Lord's will to be done. I didn't understand if I was putting too much into this interview and not letting him be in control. I was done and back to my room. Donna said that Margery had called to see if we were still coming and Donna told her the interruption that happened this morning. She said it would be fine for she was having the lawyer help her get the car started as the battery had gone dead. That made me feel like she was really planning on me to help her and I forgot all about the kidney problem. I got dressed and off we went. As we drove I was thinking we were going closer in to a housing area. Donna said they didn't have many major highways so lots of times you have to go out of the way to get to where you were going. I thought, really! Finally we stopped at the address she gave me but I thought it couldn't be here and I must have written it down wrong. Donna pulled up in the driveway and told me to go knock and find out where this address on the paper was. So I did. Knocking and then a man opened the door and asked, 'Are you Lucinda?' I replied, 'yes' and waved to Donna to come. I was still in shock as I looked around the front of the house and waited on Donna. We walked in and I shook hands with a Mr. Richards but he said, 'Call me Carl'. I looked behind him at a pretty little lady in a wheel chair calling 'Lucinda, Lucinda,' in her faint little voice. We hugged and she said to call her Miss Margery. I then introduced Donna to both of them. Carl said that lunch was on the table so we should sit down and talk while we ate. It was so delightful and I was able to answer all her questions and even Carl's which really surprised me. I thanked the Lord while we enjoyed our. Carl wanted to talk with me so he asked me to go out on the patio that overlooked A BEACH!!!! I gasped and just kept saying, 'how beautiful, how beautiful'. Then he asked if I would like to take a walk on the beach but I told him Donna had to get back for she had just taken her lunch hour to bring me over. He said, 'I would be happy to take you back'. He continued, 'I have clients at the base so can get a pass'. I looked at my watch and said Donna probably should get back so that would be wonderful. We went in to find Donna talking to Miss Margery. Carl said to Donna that he would take me back for we do not want to make her late. She agreed and said she would see me maybe before she went home. I hugged her and thanked her for bringing me. She turned to Margery and thanked her for the lovely lunch and she left.

I went to the kitchen and said I wanted to help clean up and we could talk while we did that. Carl replied that he would help her later. They were so wonderful and felt I was who Miss Margery wanted to care of her. Carl asked when I could start so I had to tell them about my medical condition and what I was to have done every three to four weeks with blood tests. Miss Margery told me that she could have a neighbor come and stay with her while I went to have the tests done. If I needed to be hospitalized a visiting nurse could come and stay overnight with her. Carl smiled and said, 'I think we can work out whatever needs to be done for I am getting the vibes from Miss Margery that she wishes for you to live with her'. I returned the smile and added, 'I have been praying for the Lord to direct me and you both as to where God wants us'. Miss Margery told Carl to show me the house and what room I would like to call mine. There was a beautiful room at the end of the hallway that had a sitting area in it so was nice for privacy. It had its own bath outside the bedroom so was laid out very nice. We walked back down the hall to the living room and there was another guest room, smaller but nice sized. The bath was a two-way where it could be used for guests visiting or for the guest bedroom. When I got back into the living room I asked where Miss Margery's bedroom was and she pointed around the opposite way. I walked to the door as Carl watched and said, 'but she is so far from the back room, how would I hear her'. I added, 'I would rather take the other room to be closer'. He turned to Miss Margery and said, 'She passed my test'. He came over to me and put his hand on my shoulder and said, 'Not one of the other prospects thought of that and that is why I didn't hire them.' He continued and looked at Miss Margery, 'She will care for you like a daughter I know.' A tear came to my eye and I said, 'God wants me here I know that now.' I went over and hugged Miss Margery and said I would be calling her when the doctors tell me I can be dismissed. I added, 'I pray it is soon.' As we drove back I asked Carl where her children lived and he said she has none and all of their families are gone. I asked him how long he had been taking care of her and he said for seven years when she developed rheumatoid arthritis and kidney problems. He said she had gone in twice for kidney failure and had dialysis then, adding that it had been about six months since her last one. He left me at the curb and drove off.

## Chapter 19

## Home For Christmas

As I waved goodbye to Mr. Richards I walked in the hospital and back to my room. I was excited but found myself pretty tired. Donna had gone and Nancy said she was to call Dr Connor when I returned. Dr Connor called and said they were going to give me a dose of antibiotics for something was going on with my left kidney and the sonogram showed it to be swollen, much larger than my right kidney. He said it could be a parasite that lodged in there and causing an infection so for tonight I would be on an IV of antibiotics. He said that Dr Hartman had called and would be calling me in the morning. I told him thank you and to say hello to Heather. I wasn't hungry after that nice lunch at Miss Margery's so didn't go and see if anyone was in the cafeteria. It was only 6 o'clock, but I thought I would watch TV and wait for Nancy to bring in the IV and get me hooked up for the night. I must have fallen asleep for Nancy was touching my arm and said she was ready to put the IV in. When she left I turned out the lights but left the TV on but couldn't stay awake.

The phone woke me up and I looked at the clock and it was 7 o'clock. I answered to find Dr Hartman calling me. He asked how my interview went. After telling him all about the house and how they would work with the tests and stuff here at the hospital he was relieved to hear that. We talked about the kidney problem and he thought it might be the same thing as Dr Connor had thought. He was sure the antibiotics would take care of it for sometimes that happened and a dead parasite gets stuck in the tissue and causes infection. Especially since my immune system was weak it couldn't fight that hard.

He asked me what I was doing for Christmas and I told him that I was hoping he would come home. Only a month away and he would come for the week. I was so happy and asked if we could take a few days and get a way. I told him I was so ready to be with him. He told me that Dr Connor was going to dismiss me next week and said I could stay at his house if I wanted too. He wanted me to be there when he came back but I wasn't sure if Margery could wait that long. I told him I would call her and see if the first of the year would be fine. You wanted to make sure I was rid of the infection and my blood had built up better. He agreed that would be a great idea.

I went down to the cafeteria for breakfast and when I got back to my room Dr Connor had just walked in. He said he wanted to push one more dose of antibiotic in me over night and thinks that will do it. He said, 'your temperature is going down so we think that one more will do the trick. He said Dr Hartman had called and gave me the good news of him coming home for Christmas and knew I would be happy.

Calling Miss Margery was not going to be easy but I prayed and hoped she would understand and realize it was just a few weeks away. Of course when she heard my voice she was hoping I was telling her I was coming now. I told her of the kidney situation and she said, 'you stay right there and get all well before you come'. I thanked her and told her she could call me anytime.

As I was packing I thought, 'Only 2 weeks before Guy gets home and I wanted to make it a great week. I had planned on what I would fix for meals and how I would make them all special. He loved take-out Chinese so I knew I was going to make him that. I called Heather and told her I was all packed and ready so she came up and got me. I took my things in and went back over to Heathers as she had fixed some tea for us. When I opened the door Honey was jumping all over me. Drinking our tea we talked about Miss Margery and where she lived and I mentioned what a great lawyer she had who was very caring for her. I was excited to be moving into Guy's house and wanted to fix dinner for her and Perry. She said, 'maybe we can share recipes!' I looked forward to have my best friend be right across the street. I told her about Guy's phone call and asked her if she thought the neighbors would put us down for me wanting to stay here with Guy for the week he was home. She thought that many of the neighbors go to the states for Christmas so didn't think anyone would know. She was happy and as much as she liked Guy she said she was left out a lot but with me there we would be a foursome. I told her we were going somewhere for a couple of days and she understood for we really never had a lot of time alone. I went back over to the house and put my things in Bret's room.

I found myself really tearing into his house cleaning it from top to bottom. I thought he said he had a lady who came in and cleaned, but he must have let her go for it was very dusty. I went to bed very exhausted but set the alarm to call Bonnie in the am hours. Bonnie was so happy for me as I told her all about Miss Margery's house and I was going to ask her about her coming for the summer. She had that big bedroom and Bonnie would love it. I had to wait to feel her out before mentioning it.

He will be home in a week and will come home to a very clean house. I felt very good that he would appreciate it. He was calling me every night!!! I did not tell him what I had done nor did I ask him about his cleaning lady. It was time for another blood work up at the hospital so I walked down after showering for they said to not eat. It was great to see Donna so visited with her until they told me to go down to the lab. Dr Connors heard me as I was talking to the technician and asked how I was doing and I told him I was feeling great. He said Heather had told him of my tearing into cleaning Guy's house and he cautioned me that I should not overdo it this soon. He said, 'I know you have energy now but with Guy coming home you don't want to get sick.' I assured him I was done and I was just relaxing and visiting with Heather until he came. I got the thumbs up again and he walked out. I went down to see Donna again and told her she ought to come down and visit on her lunch break this week.

I walked back to the house and fixed some breakfast and picked up one of Guys' books to read. I turned on the radio and was listening to some 50's music for thought I could get exercise by dancing. Heather knocked at the door and said she was going to the commissary to get some groceries for their Christmas dinner and asked if I wanted to go with her. I thanked her for I needed to get some things too. I then asked, 'How about you two coming to Guy's house for dinner'? She told me that her sister from Nebraska was coming and bringing their four children. I told her maybe after they leave we could plan something. She agreed and as we walked into the commissary we parted ways with our carts.

That evening Guy called and I asked him who was picking him up at the terminal and he said the motor pool has a shuttle and would bring him home. He asked, 'Are you counting the days like I am?' I replied, 'Over and over all day long'. I told him that the Connor couldn't come for Christmas dinner because they had company coming. He reminded me that we were going away and we would be spending Christmas away. I said, 'Oh, I did not know. He said, 'I wanted it to be a surprise but where I am taking you will be.'

I got out of bed and started jumping up and down and kept singing, 'tomorrow, tomorrow, I can't wait until tomorrow.' For some reason the day went so slow and I just couldn't stop thinking about it. The phone rang and it was Donna telling me she would like to come down on her lunch break. I was so happy for it would help me pass the time. I hurriedly put a chicken breast in the skillet and fixed a tossed salad. Setting the table I heard a knock and let Donna in. Told her to sit for the chicken wasn't quite ready. I asked her what she was doing for Christmas, as I was ashamed of myself for not asking her before. She said they were all going back to Colorado to ski with her in-laws. They had a cabin and they go there almost every year. The chicken is done and salad ready to eat. We sat and talked about her family and it was so great for it seemed it was always hospital staff or things to do with the hospital that we only talked about. She was so happy that I was going to move into that beautiful beach front house. I told her that maybe Miss Margery would let her come and have lunch with us some day. She commented that she would love it. She got up and said she needed to get back to work. I wished her a Merry Christmas for they were leaving the end of the week for Colorado.

I turned on the radio and had it on the 50's-60's station and exercised until I was sweating with the 'oldies'! I jumped in the shower and thought I would be tired enough to fall asleep but found I was too excited so got a book and started reading. That always does the trick and when I woke up it was 2 am so turned out the light and fell back to sleep.

Waking up singing, 'This is the day, this is the day, and this is the day that the Lord is bringing Guy home.' Praying to the Lord that of course this is His day also and I thank him for it. Guy didn't call last night but he said it would be in around lunch time. Heather was to pick up her family at the airport today but at the civilian airport. I had packed a bag for 2 or 3 days so was ready as I wasn't sure what day we were going. Christmas was three days away and he said we would be gone over Christmas.

I pulled his car out of the garage and decided to wash it as it was dusty also. I was sure we would be taking it instead of the truck. He would be surprised but maybe not even notice for it had been in the garage all this time.

I called Miss Margery to see how she was doing and she sounded great. She said that Carl was taking her out for Christmas to a restaurant and she was looking forward to that. I told her I would be having dinner with the doctor for he had no family coming. We talked for a while and then told her I had to go. I was sweaty from washing the car so jumped in the shower again and put on my long floral skirt and a pretty blouse that flowed. I was ready for him to come home anytime. I turned on the radio to listen to pass the time. I didn't want to dance and exercise for I would get all sweaty again so I just danced slow and visualized Guy there with me. I loved to sing along with the music as my sister and I used to dance together and sing. The boys at school just weren't dancers so most of the girls would dance together. We loved to roller skate and take some of the steps we learned and dance to them. It was so much fun. I guess the radio was too loud for I had not heard the door open and was just swaying with the music and singing. All of a sudden two arms went around my waist and started dancing with me. I turned and jumped in his arms and we finished the song that way. I asked, 'How is it that you always come in when I am dancing'? We couldn't stop kissing and then the phone took care of that. It was Perry asking us to come over and meet Heather's sister and have a glass of wine. We looked at each other and he said, 'We are leaving as soon as I empty out my dirty clothes and put some clean ones together and I promise you we won't be interrupted again'. We laughed and ran across the street to the Connors.

Driving to our hotel Guy kept telling me he was going crazy not having me there with him. He said he was hoping that I could come to California where he was and on week-ends we could drive to see Bonnie. I told him I wanted to be with him too but wanted to take more time in getting to know him. We had not really been together except in the hospital surroundings. He understood and was hoping they would not make him stay there as long as he was told. Dr Perry was doing a great job here and easily was handling the entire work load. His practice was being shared by all the rest of the doctors so he could do the duties of hospital commander that Guy was doing.

We talked about meeting Miss Margery but he wanted to be with me for he could meet her on the next trip. I told him about her needing kidney dialysis about every four months. He didn't think that was a good sign so I questioned him about the signs that I needed to look out for and when I needed to call for the paramedics. I had taken my journal tablet so had paper to write directions down and thankful that I had done that.

We got to the hotel and checked in as it was getting evening and he had made dinner reservations. We changed clothes not giving in to the temptation of staying in. I knew he had an agenda so wanted it to go as he had planned. Going down the elevator he held me and we both laughed for we knew to cool it or we would be heading back up to our room.

The dining room was so beautiful and they placed us by the window to look out at the ocean. The sun was just going down and I looked at him and asked, 'Did you plan that too?' He smiled and said, 'All for you'. I leaned over and we kissed. He was grinning with the same look that he gets when he is up to something and I gave him a questionable smile back. Then he just laughed. We ordered and while we waited they brought a bottle of wine. I don't think we stopped talking when they brought our dinner. We had so much to talk about and I wanted him to know everything. I was sure of some things we mentioned on the phone but he always called right before he had to turn in.

The next two days were filled with just ourselves and enjoying being free to feel what our hearts had been feeling but afraid to show it in the hospital environment. He told me all about his family and I shared about mine. It was so sweet that he wanted to drive across the country to see all of our families. My heart was making no mistakes in feeling he loved me in a very serious way. We both knew we couldn't talk about the future as he wasn't sure where he was going to be sent and didn't want me to sit in Hawaii waiting. He was glad I was getting a job to pass my time.

Christmas night we went to another hotel for dinner and when we drove up I knew we couldn't have afforded to stay there but maybe eating wasn't too bad. We were seated and as I looked around I noticed they had a pianist and dance floor. I really got excited for I would love to know how to play the piano. My mother wanted the girls to learn and did some washing for our school music director for my oldest sister to have lessons. She was very talented in the music field so that was fine with me. We ordered and the waiter told us that the pianist would play anything we wanted to hear. Guy and I started saying some songs of the 60's that we loved, like, *Theme from a Summer Place* and *The Magic Touch*. We were just naming one after the other out loud and agreeing with each other that we liked that one and that one. Finally Guy got up and went over to the man and then came back and asked me to dance. He started playing, *Theme from a Summer Place* and I just melted in his arms. He is such a smooth dancer and it was so easy to just float around with him. I could have danced all night but we saw our dinner arrive so went to eat. I was so full but excused myself to go to the ladies room and freshen up my make-up. When I came back the tables were cleared and he had poured me another glass of wine. I told him two would be my limit for I can smell the cork and get tipsy sometimes. He took my hand in his as the pianist start playing *At Last* and Guy went down on one knee beside me and I looked into his beautiful eyes for I heard him tell me about the night he came into my room and got flustered in talking to me and I was just smiling back at him and he knew then that He feel in love with me. He said I never am lost for words but with you and looking at you and how beautiful you were I was smitten. Then he said, 'Now that I can't be without you in my life and love you more than myself and can't think of living without you, so you would please complete my life and marry me?' I took his face in my hands and with tears running down my cheeks I leaned down and kissed him and said, 'Yes, yes, yes'. Putting a ring on my finger and then pulling me up. He took me in his arms and led me to the dance floor while the man continued to play. I think I heard someone applauding but I could not take my eyes off the most wonderful man I had ever known. Then he whispered in my ear, 'Let's go to our room'.

I can not put into words the love that this man showed me during those few days we had together. As soon as we arrived back on base we went across the street to our dear friends home and told them the news. Both Perry and Heather gave us hugs, as in a group hug. It was so exciting that we could finally tell people about our love for each other. Perry told Guy that he was sorry but so proud of the way he had handled it all for they knew just by being in the same room with us how we felt toward each other. Perry said, 'Every morning I noticed Guy coming in the back door and stopping off to see how your night went and then every night before he left the hospital he came in to say goodnight to you. Maybe no one else noticed but I did and thought it was about time for Guy to come out of his shell and not be afraid of letting a woman into his life again.' Perry went to their cabinet and brought out a bottle of champagne. He said, 'Heather thought we ought to buy this for we both felt this was going to be a special week for you two and we wanted to be a part of your celebration'. Of course tears were coming down my face and Heather came over and hugged me.

Guy and Perry went out on the patio to talk and Heather and I went into the kitchen. Her sister had just left and had tons of dishes so I started helping her clean up. We both wondered what the men were talking about and I felt it must be important for them to go out by themselves. I asked Heather if there was a case at the hospital that Perry needed advise on, but she didn't know for Perry had not said anything.

The guys came back in and Guy asked me if I was ready to go to the house and of course I said yes. Guy told Perry he would see him down at the office in the morning so Heather and I looked at each other and raised our eyebrows.

I couldn't believe what my heart was feeling as I stood at the door waving goodbye to Guy as the shuttle bus drove off. What was I going to do without him? I ran back in and fell on the sofa just sobbing for I didn't know when I would see him again. I finally got up as someone was tapping on the door and when I opened it I found Heather just looking at me. I opened the door I just feel on her shoulder crying. She went to the stove to put on some hot water for tea and fixed us a cup. We spent the day just hanging out, walking and talking.

# Chapter 20

# My New Home For Now

Three months have already gone by and I was adjusting in my new home and caring for Miss Margery. She was truly a blessing and I felt so close to her as if she was mentoring me. I loved my mother with all my heart but she was trying to raise 6 kids and put up with my alcoholic father. I knew she wouldn't tell me if he was still beating her and I wanted to see her so bad. Miss Margery played the piano and we would sing a lot. She had a little Bible church down the street where she used to go and played for them. Carl could not come and get her every week and take her so I was excited to be able to. I have gotten a license so she was able to go with me. We would sing together for she would sing alto and I would sing the melody. She is so easy to care for!

Guy has made the trip home each time I have had to go in for my six week stay in the hospital for a blood transfusion. My kidney is doing so much better and on those stays I am given antibiotics in a light dose just to help the infection that I had and to ward off any other infection with my immune system weak. He loves Miss Margery and I did not know he had such a great voice so we spent time together singing old hymns. I can tell it excites Miss Margery. He usually has to fly out on Sunday so never really gets to go to church. He loves running and walking on the beach. We find time to do that when Miss Margery is taking a nap. Sometimes she wheels out on the patio and watches us.

Only a few more months and Bonnie will be out for summer break. She is planning on coming and Miss Margery has promised her the back bedroom for her enjoyment and privacy. I know she will love it and if she wants to come her junior year Margery said she would love to have a granddaughter live here.

It is Saturday and I called my sister this morning to see how all the families were back home. They are all hard workers and have families so not sure if they have the money to fly to Hawaii. I can not leave Miss Margery so someday we will have a reunion.

Miss Margery and I are working on making a quilt for Guy and myself when we start our life together. She has such beautiful material and it has been so much fun. Some of the ladies from church are coming once a week to help us quilt it. They have a meeting once a month and the other weeks we work on quilts then have our pot-luck lunch and work again until about two. It is so much fun to see how Miss Margery has blossomed in these last few months and Guy said I had brought life back into her. She deserves it for she has been a wonderful blessing to so many in her life time.

As Miss Margery and I were eating lunch Guy called and wants me to fly over and attend a Spring Officer Ball at the Club there next month. I was so excited but wasn't sure I would be able to do it. I told him I would check with Carl and see if we could get a visiting nurse to come in for a week. I was sure it would be no problem and I wanted to go so bad. Miss Margery heard our conversation so when we hung up I told her what he wanted and she got so excited and said she had many formals that I could choose from. She got on the phone and called Carl to tell him to line it up for the dates Guy wanted me to come. I started crying for I wanted to see Bonnie again too. I knew I would be seeing her this summer so thought I could drive up there while Guy was at work.

Monday came and I had to go and get my four week blood work done at the hospital. One of the ladies from the church came to sit with Miss Margery while I was gone. It is always so good to see my friends and Heather comes down and sits with me while I am there. I told her about Guy's call and she was so excited for me. Heather said I should ask Nancy for she was single and just might like to stay with Miss Margery and she could use the money. I thought that would be a great idea but would have to check with Miss Margery before asking Nancy. I got her number from Donna and went back home. I mentioned to Miss Margery about having a nurse that I knew and trusted to come stay with her. She said she could pay her and would love to have her come. I called Nancy to see if she could take leave for a week and come and stay with her and she was so excited to take some vacation time and get paid to care for Miss Margery. I told her to try and come over after work, for she worked from 11pm to 7am. She was so sweet and said she could come over on Saturday for she lived in the barracks. I know that would be a better time for Miss Margery too. That way she could meet her and just see if she would like to do it before saying yes.

I got off the phone because Miss Margery was calling me from the back bedroom. I got scared for I thought she had fallen out of her wheel chair but she was looking in the larger wardrobe closet and her voice just sounded different. She pointed to some boxes at the top and also some clothes garment bags and said to get them down for they had formals in them. She said, 'We will have to get to work on finding you the perfect one that will make Colonel Guy's eyes pop out'. We just laughed and as I laid them on the bed she picked through them and would say, 'No, not that one, maybe this one, oh yes, this one'. Pulling out the skirt part she had me pull the whole dress out. By the time we had gone through five bags and boxes I had 12 dresses to look at. She said now go and try these on for if we have to make modifications on them we need to do it right away. She rolled out to the dining room while I was trying on the dresses. They were so beautiful and I felt like it was all a dream that I had this many to try on let alone going to a BALL! Miss Margery came back in with a pad and pencil in her hand saying, 'I will put down the dress that we like the best and then figure out the accessories to go with it'. As I tried on each dress I was eager to wear certain ones but Miss Margery would say, 'No that is not the one'. Finally, I tried on a beautiful light turquoise colored long dress and put it on. At first I couldn't figure it out for it was off the shoulder on the right arm with no sleeve and a ruffled flower on the sleeve of the left shoulder. It looked something like a flamingo dancer gown that was so soft and had a slit on the right side but full of ruffles around the slit and they went all around the bottom of the skirt. It was so beautiful and when I walked out Miss Margery gasped and put her hand to her mouth and said, 'That's the one'. I felt very sexy in it but told her I thought I should have one more that was more conservative in case he didn't like the first one. She agreed so we kept on looking. Finally, I pulled out a black chiffon strapless that was gathered at the top and flowed from an empire waist to the floor. It was very elegant looking and Miss Margery felt if he liked black he would adore this one. She said, 'Honey, you look pretty pale in it but it is beautiful on you'. She added, 'Why don't you get some sun, and do it a little each day to make you tan and maybe that will help. So while I put all the dresses back in their garment bags she went into the living room. When I went out she was writing down what accessories would look great with the dresses. She said, 'Your feet are too small so you can not wear any of my shoes, so we will have to buy you some to go with either of the dresses. She asked me to go in and bring in her large jewelry box and also a drawer that had boxes of jewelry in it. I laid the dresses across the sofa and she would take out piece after piece to see what I should wear with it. While she did that I started to work on finding something for dinner.

## Chapter 21

# Not Miss Margery Lord

As I got out of bed and got dressed I did my usual trip to look in on Miss Margery and to help her get in the shower I noticed she was still asleep. It wasn't like her for she liked to read her Bible first thing before I came in. I said laughing, 'did I wear you out yesterday with all that preparation on my dresses?' She opened her eyes with a stare and I knew something was wrong. I tried to get her to answer me but she couldn't get any words out. I immediately called 911 and then called Carl. I called Guy right away and told him what was happening and what should I do. He said to give her one of her baby aspirins and raise her pillow up to where she is sitting against the head board. I no sooner had done that than the ambulance was there and within the time they were helping Miss Margery Carl came.

I told Carl that I would drive as I was going to stay there with her and he could leave anytime he wanted so we drove separately to the hospital.

I wanted to be with Miss Margery when we got to the emergency room but they had Carl and I wait in the waiting room. I was getting very tearful and just kept saying, 'I can't loose her, not now'. Carl put his arm around my shoulder and said, 'She thinks of you as her daughter and I know you have become very close to her too'. He went on, 'She is tough but she will be alright, just pray and trust'. We both sat and prayed until I looked up and saw Dr Perry coming in. I jumped up and walked to him. He put his arms around me and said that Guy had called and he was on his way down town anyway but wanted to come by to see if there was anything he could do. I had tears in my eyes and said they had not come out yet to tell us what was going on. Just then I heard the door open and a doctor came over to us and said Miss Margery had suffered a major stroke but they are running a bunch of tests to see how much damage it caused. I started crying and Carl came over as Dr Perry was asking the ER doctor some medical questions. He took Dr Perry in and turned to us and said they would be back. I was so thankful because I knew Dr Perry would get the information to help me understand how bad it was. A nurse came out and I asked her if we could go in and see Miss Margery but she said we would have to wait for just a little while longer. We sat down and waited until Dr Perry came out. I introduced him to Carl and he said that Miss Margery was not able to communicate right now so we should go home. I didn't want to but he informed me there was nothing I could do and she wouldn't even know I was there. Carl said he wanted to wait and talk to the doctor and I agreed. I hugged Dr Perry and he said he would call Guy and I would probably hear from him tonight. Carl and I waited until the doctor came out and told us that he would call us if she showed any sign of understanding where she was. We left and drove home. Carl came in and I poured us some tea and just sat there staring at the phone. Then he said that Miss Margery had him change her Will just a week ago for she just felt she needed to get her affairs in order. I said, 'But she has been feeling so great and doing so much more than she has in a long time.' He said that he had talked to her doctor when she had that last episode with her kidneys and he told him that her heart was wearing out and full of fluid. I knew that and knew she was taking a diuretic to help with that. Guy had told me to keep an eye on her feet to make sure they were not swelling and I had not seen that. Carl said, 'She told him she was ready for she missed Herman so much'. They had been married 56 years and with no children they just had each other. I asked him, 'Why didn't she share that with me?' All he could think of was that she didn't want you to worry and she loved having you here so much that she didn't worry about herself. He said she told him she wanted to make a home for Lucinda and her daughter and didn't want us to worry about me working. 'She knew you and Colonel Hartman was getting married someday but saw how much you loved the beach and her home that she didn't know who else would enjoy it more', he said. I started crying and then he said, 'I could have sold it and made lots of money on it if you had not come into her life for I was the beneficiary of her estate'. I looked up with wide eyes and saw he had tears in his eyes and then he said, 'but I agreed with her and knew the Lord would want this too'. He went on to say, 'I felt something for you the first time I saw you but at my age I knew a young woman like you needed someone her own age'.

The phone rang as we were talking and it was Miss Margery's doctor saying she had another stroke and they couldn't pull her out of it. I dropped the phone and started sobbing hysterically and didn't realize Carl had picked it up and was talking to the doctor. He came over and we cried together until I finally got control and turned to him and said, 'Now what am I going to do without her?' He said he was going to have to go to the hospital and make arrangements so would come back if I needed him. I said, 'Just call me later for I am going to call Heather and see if she will come. I asked him what I could do and he told me to call the church and those people that you think Margery wanted to know. I told him I would.

I tried to call Dr Perry but he was not in so left a message and then called Heather and she said she would come right over. I hung up and called Guy right away. He said he would be on the next plane. I was so relieved for I needed him so bad to hold me. Calling the pastor was hard but he said he was going to go to the hospital and check with Carl to see what they could do to help. He gave me the number of the ladies group who heads up the funeral meal. I called and told her I would have to get back with her as I didn't have a date yet or anything for the services.

I put on some water for tea as Heather should be here any time. I had not gone into Miss Margery's room since I had been home so went in and cried as I sat on the bed and visualized her being there. Talking as if she was there I promised her I would care for her home like she would and said thank you for treating me like your daughter. I went on to tell her I cherished every moment I had with her and promised that I would think of her in every room I walked through. I looked down at her night stand and saw a paper sticking out and went to open it and push it back but noticed it said, Last Will and Testament. I opened it up and it spelled out all that she was designating to Carl and me. I was reading it when I heard the whistle of the tea pot so folded it up and took it with me. I turned off the water and walked to my bedroom and sat on the bed to finish reading it. With tears rolling down my face I could not believe what I was reading. She had only given Carl her stocks in a company that I had not heard of but the rest of the entire estate went to me. I quickly put it in my dresser drawer as I heard knocking and knew it must be Heather. When I opened it she just grabbed me and held me as I started crying again. We walked and sat on the sofa and talked about it all and then I remembered that I was going to make tea. I just had to keep busy and forget the Will that I had just looked at. Heather had not seen the house so I took her through it and we walked outside to look down the beach. The house set back and there was a long stair way leading up and down from the beach. So we just sat on the steps and watched the waves come in and out. Finally she said, 'Do you want me to stay the night with you? I quickly answered, 'No, I am pretty sure I will be fine, but thank you so very much'. I jumped up as the phone was ringing and found Dr Perry on the other end. He asked if he needed to come over and I told him that Heather was here and I would be fine but thank you anyway. Heather had followed me in the house and I realized she had been there for about three hours so told her I would be fine and gave her a kiss and hug and she left.

Sleeping was so very hard but finally the sun woke me as it was shining in my room. I didn't get up to watch it come up as I usually did. I walked to the kitchen and fixed a cup of tea and had a banana but wasn't feeling like eating much. I went back into Miss Margery's bedroom and started stripping the bedding from her bed. While they were washing I disinfected her bath room and opened her curtain all the way. Opening the patio door that she had I wanted to air it out. It was about 11 o'clock and the doorbell was ringing. It was Carl and he wanted to go over the funeral arrangements so we sat at the table and talked. He said that Miss Margery wanted to be cremated so had taken care of that and we could pick up her remains in a couple of days. I asked, 'who will get them?' and Carl said, 'It is up to you but I thought maybe I could get my friend who is a pilot to sprinkle them along the beach here in front of her house.' 'That is a wonderful idea', I told him. He said that the pastor and he went over the order of service and it would be this Friday. 'Oh, that is just two days away'. He felt we shouldn't wait as there was no family that would be coming so I agreed. I asked him to sit down for I wanted to show him something. I went into the bedroom and got the Will and brought it out and handed it to him. He looked at it and said, 'Oh, this is her copy and it is up-to-date as you can see'. I looked at him and then ask, 'Are you okay with what it says?' He responded, 'Very much so for I know you have been like a real daughter to her'. He continued to say, 'Margery paid him a great salary to be her financial advisor, caretaker and lawyer, plus leaving me a stock in one of the fastest growing companies in the world'. He finished by saying, 'I feel very humbled for what she has done for me'. I was so thankful for I didn't want Carl to think in this short time of being with her that she gave me more. How awesome our Lord is to make everyone contented with the provisions he gives us.

He left me a copy of the funeral arrangements and left. I went in to take the bedding out of the dryer and made her bed up. It looked so clean and smelled so fresh from the ocean breeze coming in. Cleaning up the rest of her room I thought I would get a carpet cleaner to come in next week and do the whole house. She had mentioned she was going to do that anyway.

As I came out of the shower I put on a lounging dress and went to look in the freezer to see what I could fix for a meal if Guy came in today or tomorrow. I had left a message as to when the memorial would be for Miss Margery but he had not called me back. Figuring he was busy trying to wrap some things up before he came. Shutting the door of the freezer I looked up and there was the sweetest man standing with his arms open wide. I ran to them and he picked me up and carried me to the sofa as I cried in his arms. He just kept kissing me and my tears and finally he said, 'I am so sorry that you had to go through this without me'. I told him, 'Carl said that Miss Margery told him if this was to ever happen that he was to take responsibility and do it so I wouldn't have to'. I continued, 'He did and we are going to have her ashes spread out along the beach'. I looked up at him and said, 'I am fine now that you are here'. We just sat holding each other and then he said, 'Let's go for a walk on the beach for we always have to go quickly and be back'. I said, 'Miss Margery would want us to do that!'

# Chapter 22

## "Let's Go Get Married"

Today would be a sad day for I was not ready to say goodbye to Miss Margery but thankful that I would be starting my new life with a man I loved dearly. I opened my eyes and Guy was standing looking out the patio window drinking a cup of coffee. I got out of bed and put my arms around his waist and he took one of my hands and kissed it as he continued to look out at the beautiful sunrise. Then he said, 'Let's go get married'. I surprisingly looked at him and said, 'Now'? Then added, 'the memorial service is at 1 o'clock so would we be back in time'? He said, 'We still can do that but I just want you to be my wife now and be blessed by God for what we are doing cannot make him pleased with us'. I threw my arms around him and said, I would be so proud to marry you this instant to be right with our Lord'. He went to the phone and called Chaplain Fergus and told him what we wanted to do and all about Miss Margery's memorial service. I heard Guy laugh and he said we would be there as soon as we go to the court house and thanked him for calling ahead for us. Then he called Perry and Heather to see if they could come and stand up for us at the chapel. They of course were so excited to be a part of our glorious moment.

I got dressed in a pretty little flowered dress and Guy put on some slacks and we left to drive down town. I turned to him and asked him if he brought the ring and he said, 'Oh, yes for sure'. Arriving at the court house we almost ran in for Guy said we might get it today but most have to wait twenty-four hours. It all depended on the work load. He said, 'Chaplain Fergus would plead about Guy having to leave and go to another base, which was not a lie, and so needed it right away. We went to the clerk and told her who we were and she told us Judge Curtis was waiting on us. We walked in and he shook hands with Guy and asked, 'Is this what you are here for and handed Guy the license. We thanked him and turned to leave hearing Judge Curtis say, 'Congratulations'. Off we went to the base and all of a sudden we both started laughing and singing along with the radio. What a beautiful day God has made for us.

As we walked into the chapel Chaplain Fergus was there to meet us and hugged both Guy and myself. He told us that this was his first experience with marrying a couple with this mind set and was so honored to do it and thanked us for honoring the Lord this way. Guy handed him the license and told him the Connors were coming to stand up with us so they would be witnesses to sign our license.

I didn't have the wedding dress that I had dreamed of wearing but I had the love of my life marrying me and I felt just as pretty standing there with him as we looked into each other's eyes. We said our vows and when we kissed I cried as he held me so tight in his arms. Chaplain Fergus hugged us again and told us that he felt the presence of God here and had watery eyes as he told us. We turned to Perry and Heather to sign the license and off we went to our home on the beach to start our new life together.

On the way to the house Guy said, 'We can have a reception and do this over, then have the wedding you wanted. I told him the reception is all I wanted so we could have one in the states for the families there and then one here at the base so our friends here could celebrate with us. We drove up to the house and he drove the car into the garage for he was always a gentleman and opened the car door for me but this time when he did he picked me up and carried me through the door. I felt so brand new as he held me and when he let go of me he said, 'Don't you feel different'? He continued with, 'What do you think about Perry and Heather watching the house so you can come to California with me'? He added, 'They could come and stay whenever they wanted'. I thought it was a great idea so would ask them today.

It was now noon and we had to get to the church for I wanted to help Carl if there was something I could do. Pulling up, the florist was taking in flowers and saw Carl helping. We both walked over and grabbed some from the truck and carried them in. The funeral home people were there arranging them and Carl asked if I would like to say anything and I told him I would be honored if I didn't start crying. I walked back to the baptistery room and sat there in private trying to put together something to say. I prayed for the Lord to help me and to make it where I would not get too emotional and not be able to finish. I thanked Him and walked out to join Guy. As Carl and I sat in the back where people were coming in and thanked them for coming. Then I looked up and tears filled my eyes as Dr Perry, Heather and many of the staff from the hospital was walking in. I was so pleased and hugged them and pointed to where Guy was sitting, so they went to join him.

Miss Margery's service was so sweet with the music; testimonies and even mine went well. Her pastor talked about all she had done for the church for so many years. I said to myself I felt she was in heaven looking down singing along with us. The pastor commented about me coming into her life and seeing the joy coming back into her spirit so he knew God had brought me to her. He continued to say that even though we didn't have a long time to be together, it was all in God's timing and he wanted to reward Margery with something precious in her last days on earth. I had tears streaming down my cheeks and Guy put his arm around me and held me against him. What comfort to have someone there reminding me that he is there and will be for the rest of my life.

We said our thanks and goodbyes to the staff and church families but then asked Perry and Heather if they could come by for a short time to talk to us. They laughed and reminded us that this was our honeymoon night. I said, 'Who better than you two to spend part of it with'. Guy agreed and we started home.

We went into the house and Guy went to the fridge and pulled out a bottle of wine. He said, "This is not Champagne but we can pretend'. As we went into the living room Perry stood up and toasted Guy and I and asked if he could pray for our marriage. I was so touched for I had never seen anyone pray at a toasting. Thanking him, Guy then started talking to them about our plans, for how he wanted me with him in California. 'What would you two think if we offered you the house while we are gone? You could stay every weekend or anytime you wanted'? They loved the beach and took no time in saying that they would love to do it. Then Heather said, 'You can let us know when you plan to come back and we will vacate'. We laughed and said thank you so much. Guy said we had to leave Tuesday so that gave us three more days here. I said, 'Why don't you come over after church and we can show you around and Guy can show you where all the shut-offs are located'.

After the Connor's left Guy asked me to sit down with him and he told me that he had five months left on the enlistment through the reserves and that he wasn't sure if he wanted to sign up again or go into private practice here.

'I will call Monday and get an appointment with a doctor friend of mine at the community hospital in Honolulu and see what my chances are here'. He looked at me and I told him I know he loves it here in Hawaii and we do have a home free and clear so do we take it as a sign that God had plans for us to stay here. I went on to say, 'I would do whatever the Lord's will was but now you are the head of this house and I am to honor that'. He took me in his arms and said, 'I will never make any plans without talking them over with my wife, ever'.

The next morning we knew that since it was Saturday we wanted to call all the families and tell them of our marriage, especially Bonnie. I could see her more often until we came back to Hawaii to live. We finished our breakfast which was a treat for me as I could now cook for my husband all the time. Knowing that he loves to cook he commented that we could take turns. Wow, I thought, for I never had a husband that wanted to help in the kitchen. I told Guy that the girls and I had fun in the kitchen cooking.

Finishing breakfast we each went to a phone so we could both talk, first calling his mother and dad and hoping that Bret would still be hanging around the house. His mom, Barbara answered and Guy said, 'Mom I called to see if you and Dad are going to be home sometime next month and have no travel plans'? Barbara answered with, 'No, son, I can't think of any plans right now, why do you ask'? Guy lovingly replied, 'Well, I was thinking of bringing your new daughter-in-law up to meet you'. There was silence and then with a sobbing sound she said, 'Is it Lucinda'? Guy answered, 'Yes, it is'. Then I heard Guy's dad, 'Hey, is she on the line too'? So I answered, 'Yes, I am and hello'. They both said, 'Congratulations you two we have been wondering when we would get this call'. Barbara said to me, 'Lucinda, we feel we already know you by the conversations we have had with Guy'. Feeling very shy I responded, 'I am looking so forward in coming to Oregon to meet you both and Bret'. Richard asked, 'When did you get married'? Guy answered, 'Yesterday, for I just couldn't stand being away from her so went to the Chaplain and asked him to do it'. He added, 'We were wondering if we had a reception in June would you be able to come down for we wanted both you and Lucinda's family to come. I jumped in to say that the youngest daughter wanted to come and stay with us during her summer break so I would probably come back here with her until Guy could come home possibly permanently. It was a very sweet phone call and I felt like I really was welcome in the family.

Calling Bonnie was different as her step mom answered the phone and at first told me she was sleeping and she didn't want to wake her. I tried not to lose my cool and then told her I needed to talk to her as this was an emergency! I knew the Lord would not be angry with me, for to me it was, but I wanted her to know right away. When Bonnie came on the phone she was groggy but her voice livened up when she heard my voice. I knew there was a possibility that her step mom was on the phone listening but I didn't care. I said to Bonnie, Do you want to hear some wonderful news'? Then she said, 'Did you and the doctor get married'? I told her we did and she was so happy but when I told her I was moving to California with him to finish out his stay there and we would be there on Tuesday, she began to cry, but I reminded her I was coming back with her in tow to spend the summer with us in Hawaii. I told her about the reception that we were going to have in California so that his family could all come down and also hope that Grandma and my family could come. That way she would get to meet all of his family and could see her grandma, uncles and aunt's hopefully. Then she told me that she was getting her drivers permit but couldn't drive alone. I said, 'Maybe Donny and Candy would want to come'. I added, 'I would send you the money for gas and you could pay their way'. I reminded her it wasn't until sometime in June so a couple of months to plan. Guy broke in and said, 'Bonnie, we would even come and get you and then you and your mom could take off and go back home for the summer if that would help'. I told Guy, 'what a great idea honey' 'If you could come that would be wonderful, but let us know'. Guy came on and told her to write the phone number down but more than likely we would be calling you with the details. Again, I thank the Lord for a smart and thinking husband who cares and wants to be a part of her life.

Guy and I felt we needed to find where all the utility turn-offs were to tell Perry when they come over. I was so glad that Carl took the time and showed me when I moved in. I called a locksmith to come and change all the locks and garage door openers for I wasn't sure who all Miss Margery had given keys too. They were coming on Monday so that was a relief to us to have it done before we left. I trusted Carl but just didn't want him to think he still could come and go as he pleased.

I got my suitcases down and started putting the necessary clothes and things together that I wanted to take on this first trip. I knew I could buy most things I needed in the states for I still had not acquired a lot of clothes.

Miss Margery said there were boxes and boxes of clothes in the garage and I noticed many garment bags full so I would tackle that when I brought Bonnie back with me. I knew I had to put in my dress to wear to the Ball. There would not be anymore functions Guy said for the short time he had left there.

Guy came in from outside and said, 'let's go over to my place and check things out plus I want to get my tuxedo and tie'. I asked him if he wanted to see my dresses I had picked out to wear. 'Go try them on and I will tell you which one I want you to wear for me', he said. I ran to the bedroom and put the black one on first with the shoes and jewelry to match. As I came down the hall I twirled around in the hallway I was trying to catch a spark of what he was thinking. He just whistled and said it was gorgeous so I said I would take this one but had one more. Slipping on the dress and then putting on my wig that I had not worn before I pulled it back on one side I put a flower in it. Slipped on my sandal heels and jewelry then walked down the hallway dancing a rumba type step. His mouth was wide open and he came and grabbed me dancing down the hall to the living room and threw me gently on the sofa kissing me, then down my bare shoulder and told me that this is the one he wanted me to wear. He then picked me up and carried me to our bedroom to help me change clothes! As he was carrying me back I raised my hands to the ceiling and said, "Lord, thank you for this man I love'!

## Chapter 23

# What Is Happening?

Putting my feet on California soil made my heart skip a beat. I now had been gone from here for over four years. The base looked the same; however, I had only been here a few times. Guy had to buy an older car while he was there for he didn't want to transport his vehicles from Hawaii to California. They just didn't know how long he would be staying here either. He had left it in the parking lot so we loaded our suitcases and headed for the commissary. He did not have much food at his place. He said he ate his big meals at the O'Club or cafeteria at the hospital. We picked up enough to get through the week and figured we would go again on Saturday. Arriving at the quarters where he lived I found it was small but just right for the two of us to be comfortable. We unpacked before we lost our energy and then he pulled back the bedding and he crashed on the bed. I came out of the bathroom and he was waving to me to come over. It was a glorious night in our new temporary home with my wonderful husband.

I woke up to Guy showering so jumped up and went out to fix some breakfast. When he came out he was grinning and only had his towel around him. He said, 'What smells so good'? I walked over to him and put my arms around him and told him that he was the only thing I smelled. I told him to quickly get dressed or he wouldn't have time to eat so I finished putting it on the table.

He asked what did I want to do today and felt I needed to walk around the quarters and see where everything was. He gave me a map of the base so I could familiarize myself with places that I might want to go check out. He gave me the key and I promised I would be here when he got home. He hollered a Yahoo and out the door he went.

The Ball is just 3 days away and I am getting excited. Guy arrived home from work as I was finishing dinner. I had the tea water ready to sit with him for a spell and hear about his day. He went in to change into something more comfortable and I had his tea poured and on the coffee table. He had picked up a paper so was ready to unwind. As I sat there with him he put his arms around me and said, 'Now this is more like it'. He added, 'Coming home to my beautiful wife and she hands me a cup of tea and comforts me by sitting with me'. I said, 'If this is all you expect then you are very easy to please'. He laughed and said, 'Oh, for the first couple of hour's maybe'. We talked about some of his happenings at work but then he said that they were going to give out promotions at the Ball. He said they don't always do that so he wasn't sure what they have planned. I then asked him what he was going to tell them for he had only four months left of his reserve time. He didn't answer at first and said he just hadn't made up his mind for he had not heard anything back from his friend at the hospital in Honolulu. It had only been a month but maybe it was time for him to call again.

I asked Guy what his plans were after the reception here in the states but he answered that he had no plans. He had not told me if he had any leave or vacation time coming so I asked him, 'Do you get time off in the reserves'? He told me they do and he had not taken but a weekend here and weekend there. Then I asked him, 'What do you think about maybe taking our honeymoon and visiting 'my' island'? He looked at me and said, 'But didn't you say it was a dangerous place'? I said, 'yes, but for a short few days I think we can be fine'. He said he would have to think about it. I added that I would like to go before Bonnie came to stay for I certainly did not want to take her there. So if we went, it would have to be soon for August was only three months away and she might want to come sooner. He looked at me again and said, 'You are serious aren't you'? 'Yes', I added, 'but only if you want to go and not go just because I want you to'. He would think about it he said.

I woke up early and put water on for tea and waited for Guy to wake up and go get his shower. I poured my tea and went out on the patio watching the beautiful sunrise. I heard a, 'good morning sweetie' and went in to get his tea poured. He came out and asked why I was up so early. I said I am nervous about tonight and the Ball but don't know why. He kissed me on the back of the neck and went in to dress. I went out to prepare the rest of the breakfast and when he came out it was ready. He said, 'they are letting most of us off early for some of the guys have to help get the program all set up'. He went on to say that something is up for when I run into certain officers talking they stop when I walk up. I asked, 'you don't know what it could be'? Guy replied, 'Nope'. I walked him to the door and kissed him goodbye and off he went to work.

I wanted to call Heather for I had not talked to her since we left. Guy had talked to Perry about things. At 3 o'clock I called for I knew she would be home to get Perry lunch and then go to the hospital to volunteer. It was so good to hear her voice and she asked how I was doing and when I would be taking my next set of tests. I told her we had not talked about it for I was feeling fine and Guy was so busy since he got back. I mentioned the Ball being tonight and was very nervous. She told me to call her tomorrow and tell her how it went so we chatted a little more and then Guy walked in.

He sat down and told me to come and sit with him. Not thinking anything else was wrong I quickly did just that. He pulled me close and said we have to talk. Of course my heart started racing and I looked at him with concern on my face. He told me that the Commander of the hospital came to visit him today and told him they wanted to promote him and they were doing it a different way but had three openings and wanted him to have first choice on them. I think he knew I wanted to ask him something and he said, 'before you ask me, if I told them that I may not continue in the reserves, I have not. I smiled for that is exactly what I was going to ask him. He went on to tell me the choices; Korea for 7 months isolated and it would be credited as a year tour, Whiteman AFB for 4 years same status as now or back to Hickam for two more years. Since he had not heard back from his friend at Honolulu I knew this would really be a hard decision. Of course as a newlywed I didn't like the idea of him going to Korea and knew if he chose to get out he wouldn't have to worry about another isolated anyway. All I could do is say, 'Let's pray about it and if you feel you need to talk to someone why don't you call Perry'?

'I am your wife and I don't want to see you leave me that I know for sure'. I added, 'but I will support you in any of the choices that you have to make'. He put his arms around me and we sat back and he prayed for God to help him with this huge decision that he had to make. After giving it to God, he got on the phone and called Perry. I went in to shower and work on my wig for tonight. I felt he needed privacy with Perry and could tell him his heart desire since he knew Perry would really advise him.

Laying my dress on the bed with all the accessories I laid out Guy's clothes and shoes. We had to get there in just a little over an hour so started putting my makeup on when Guy walked in. He just took me in his arms and held me. I told him, 'you will make the right decision for our future and I love you and trust God and Perry to have helped you'. I felt so sorry for him and knew he would make the right decision for now that he had a wife, this would affect the two of us.

We finished dressing and he kept telling me to stay at his side for he did not want any of those hounds coming near or looking at me. I laughed and said, 'I only have eyes for you so if they are looking at me, I won't see them'. He leaned over and kissed me while putting my shawl around my shoulders, as we went out the door.

The night was going great, the food terrific and my dancing partner in better form than I can remember. All those late night dances at the hospital had paid off and I was really enjoying being with a man who loves to dance. As we walked back to our table his commander came up to him and took him off to the side. I didn't watch for I didn't want to make Guy nervous. We sat at a table with three other couples, two I had met with Guy at the hospital and one of the wives at the commissary. The other couple was just as nice and friendly so we hit is off great too. Guy came back and said all is well. I believed him and squeezed his leg under the table. He dropped his hand and took mine and we just became one in thought!

When the commander went to the podium and did the formal introductions and chatter Guy's hand became moist. I said a silent prayer and squeezed it again. Then the commander called the three officers to come to the podium for their congratulations and promotions. He mentioned that two of the officers had not given him their answer for they wanted to take the time to talk with their spouses and family. I kept my eyes on Guy just in case he would look my way for an approving smile. He was so handsome in his tux that I wished I had bought a camera when I was at the Base Exchange. Then I heard the commander say, 'Colonel Hartman what is your decision as to the acceptance of your promotion and new assignment or do you decline it'? At that moment he looked at me and said, 'My wife and I have decided that we will take the Hickam assignment for I plan to retire from the reserves and go into private practice there in Hawaii in the field of Tropical Blood Diseases for it is very limited. They need my expertise in helping our boys when they come back from areas that are filled with this type of diseases. All of a sudden people were clapping and I stood up and all around me people were standing and giving Guy a standing ovation. I had tears of pride running down my face and behind me I was handed a tissue. I turned and said, 'thank you'. Not realizing later that it was the commander's wife. My heart was skipping beats so I had to sit down. I kept saying, 'Thank you God, thank you, God'. When the commander had finished with his speech about the four officers, they all went back to their chairs. I was beaming and so was Guy for he saw the peace that only God could give me and he pulled me up and kissed me . . . . right in front of everyone. Again, people clapped. I was now embarrassed but smiled up at him and as we sat I told him I was so proud.

Later that evening, after lots of people told Guy they wished him well and that it was great to hear he was continuing in his gifted field of medicine. Guy turned to me and quietly whispered, 'Isn't God Awesome.' 'What was I so worried about', he added.

# Chapter 24

# *Are We Going to the Island?*

I was sleeping so well from the late night at the Ball. I smelled coffee and knew Guy was up. I went out and he had water heating up for tea and said, I'll fix breakfast on the weekends but I want to talk to you about something first. He pulled me over to the sofa and turned to me and said, 'Let's talk about a honeymoon trip'. I looked up and agreed, 'Okay, where'? Then he said, 'The Island, the more I have thought about it the more I am really interested in going'. He continued, 'I have read your journal and really would like to see it for myself'. He asked, 'what do we have to do to make plane reservations and then to have someone fly us to the island'? I told him I would call one of the pilots from Guam and see if they are still there and get a name of a flying company who could fly us there.

Monday morning I went through my papers to see if I could find Major Davidson or Captain Carroll's phone number there. I decided to call the base locator and ask how I could locate someone at another base. Giving me the information I was able to call Guam and remembered that Captain Carroll said he would be going to Travis but Major Davidson didn't say. Finally I got someone who could help me but they said they didn't have either of the pilots still there. I was told I could call Travis and they could help me. It took a long time as the people at Guam remembered the crash but were most helpful. I finally was able to talk to someone at Travis and they gave me the Captain's phone number. When the phone rang I started getting tears and when I heard his voice I quickly told him who I was. I could hear him gasp and right away he wanted to know how I was and where I was. We talked for some time as I shared a little of what I had been through but then told him my good news and he was so excited. He said he flies here a lot so he would love to see me and meet Guy. I told him what I wanted and asked if he had any information as to who I could call. He told me he would call Guam and get me some contacts and call me back.

Two days have gone by and I finally heard from the Captain. He asked if he could deliver the information in person for they had to bring some guys down tomorrow and he asked if he could take the flight. Of course I told him we'd be honored to have him but we didn't have but a one bedroom apartment but had four chairs at the dining table so wanted him to come for dinner. When he hung up I called Guy and left a message for him to call me. I don't usually call him so he knew it would be important. It wasn't 30 minutes and he called. I told him about Captain Carroll and he was excited to have him come.

All I have to do now is to think of what we will have for dinner and if I have everything to fix it. I didn't want to go out and eat for I wanted Guy and I to have some private time with him. I decided to just fix baked chicken and baked root veggies in the oven. Guy likes that so that is what I shall fix.

It was almost time for Guy to be getting home when I heard a tapping at the door. Guy had given me the key in case I needed to run to the store so thought it was him. I opened the door with a big smile and found Captain Carroll standing there. I threw my arms around him and I cried and he kept saying, 'I didn't think I would see you again'. I pulled away and had him come in and sit. 'I wondered where you and Major Davidson were several time and also if we would ever bump into each other'. I said. He told me his first name was David. I was glad Guy wasn't home yet as he was asking me all about what happened after I got to Hickam. I didn't really give him a day by day but he got the drift of what all I had gone through. He was so excited to hear I married my doctor. That must have been Guy's cue for he tapped at the door just when David said that. I jumped up and went to let him in. Guy noticed him getting up and coming at him and they both hugged! Guy said, 'Thanks for saving my girl'. David responded, 'It was our pleasure sir'. Right away Guy told him to call him Guy for we are brothers. I saw wet eyes form in David's eyes and he said, 'We are in God's eyes'. We laughed and both said, 'Amen'.

The men talked while I put dinner on the table. It was so great to have David and see that God takes care of his children when we trust in him. I heard him and Guy mentioning those very things as they talked. Dinner was very well received for there was not much left. I was very pleased. I picked up the dishes and told the men to go and sit where it was comfortable and I would be in to see what information David had found for us. I could do the dishes later.

As David pulled out some papers from a folder he was carrying, he started showing Guy that the Wake Islands are between Guam and Hawaii but that there are smaller islands that we feel is where the plane crashed near. For Wake Island it is in a restricted area. No civilian type transportation could take you there. The Army has a station there and that is where we were headed when our helicopter had trouble. Will, Major Davidson, and I have flown over that area trying to find that island again and we cannot find it. When we came back for the guys that time we had to almost skim along the ocean to find it. It is like it doesn't exist. I really feel that God was flying our helicopter that day in order to find Lucinda. Guy and I looked at each other and smiled for this certainly made up our minds as to whether we'd be traveling there any time soon. Again, it was the Lord saying you don't need to be there. We thanked David for coming all that way to tell us but I was so glad he did for I got to see him again. He looked at me and said,'You don't know how many times I have wanted to try and find you to see how you were doing'. I knew you were going to Hickam and should have called someone there but didn't think you would have stayed this long. I asked him if he knows where Will is now and he said he was in Germany but would see if he could get a hold of him and tell him. Of course we told him if he ever came to Hawaii even for vacation to be sure and call us for we have plenty of room to put them up. He hugged me and patted my cheek and shook Guy's hand and said goodbye.

I was sad to hear that I would never get to go visit the island but yet fine with the idea as it could have been dangerous for us anyway. I went to the kitchen and Guy turned off the lights and said it's late and took my arm and led me to the bedroom.

# Chapter 25

# The Gathering

As I was finishing up the paper-plans for our reception I called Bonnie to see if she wanted to come and help me with the preparations. She was so excited to get away earlier than planned. She said she had everything packed and a few boxes with the labels I sent her to send to the Hawaii address. She still had not told her dad she was not coming back but I told her we had all the papers signed that he would not contest to her staying if she wanted to. I somehow felt he didn't think she was really going to do it. Guy and I had talked about it and if she was ready to come we would drive up there that weekend to get her. I told her to take the boxes to the post office and get them mailed and then I would call Heather and have her pick them up and take to the house.

Picking up Bonnie was not as hard as we thought as Brad and his wife had gone to Vegas and he did not want to see me. I really felt great about that so I gave Guy a tour of the base and showed him where we had lived and kids had gone to school. It was a lot different from Hickam but the kids loved it there.

Driving back, Bonnie told us that Donny couldn't get out of class and that he had now taken a part time job. However, Becky wanted to come to show us our new little grandson. We were very thankful that they had gotten stationed at Travis AFB and it was in northern California so when we come back and drive to Oregon we can I hope stop and see them. I was really getting excited now. All of a sudden Guy and I looked at each other and said, 'hey grandma, hey grandpa'. Bonnie started laughing and thanked us for being great about everything but she feels it will change some day and all for the best.

In our quarters we have a hide-a-bed for Bonnie I would make it comfortable for her to sleep on. We knew this was temporary for as soon as we have the reception Bonnie and I are flying back to Hawaii. Guy will have only one more month himself so we won't be there too long without him. When we got into the quarters, we did not think of a closet for Bonnie so took the TV cabinet, took all the stuff out of it and put it in our bedroom. She hadn't brought but a couple of things to hang so I put them in my closet, which was Guys. We neither had much for we knew it was a temporary stay. Bonnie wanted pizza so we stopped and ordered one. She was ready for bed so Guy pulled out the bed and I made it up for her while she was in the shower. I told her that the mornings would be awkward as I would be fixing Guy breakfast so she would not get to sleep in late unless she went back to sleep in our bed after he left. She said, 'That's okay for I am used to getting up early during the week. I told her we would be going to church in the morning so she would have to be up in time to go with us. She was not opposed to that so I said we will have to get ready in shifts. Guy and I will go first and then I'll make breakfast while you are getting ready. She said great and we turned the lights off and went to our room.

Guy and I looked at each other and liked the idea of going to bed early. He had bought a new book so was anxious to start reading it. I wanted to work some more on the reception plans. So Bonnie now in bed and Guy and I settled to relax for a little while. Every now and then I would feel him looking at me and I would look up and he would lean over and kiss me! My, oh, my how I love this man!!!!

Sunday was a beautiful day. We decided to drive into town for lunch after church and go to a movie. Bonnie was telling us some great ones so as we listened we finally decided on one and hoped it was still on. It was and we enjoyed it but glad to be going back to the quarters to relax. Guy and Bonnie watched a football game and talked while I put some finishing touches on our to-do list for the reception. The commander's wife had said she would be happy to give me some references on food and services. We planned to have it at the O'Club so we didn't have to rent a hall. The club usually will work with us on catering the food so I just needed to check that out.

The date was set, Bonnie put her talent together and made beautiful invitations and they were sent out. Too bad Becky was not here to help her for she had a talent for art work too.

At last count we had received over half of the replies that showed many were coming. Thankful for my brother was bringing mother and my two sisters. I was excited to finally get to see my family. We sent out names of hotels and motels for people to call and get reservations. Guy was so fortunate that he was able to get another room so Bonnie, Becky and the baby Ryan were staying there. I got a call from Guy's mother and she wanted to help with the last minute arrangements so they were coming early.

My sister called when they got to the hotel so we jumped in the car and went right over to see them. I just couldn't stop crying as I anticipated hugging my momma after so many years. Upon seeing her face she was just as beautiful as before and just grabbed Guy and gave him a great big hug. He is tall and she could only hug his middle but he reached his head down to hug her back. We all laughed and hugged as my sisters had taken rooms in the same hotel. They had all eaten but we went to the lobby to sit and talk. I knew they were all tired and tomorrow was going to be a very busy day for me. I was so thankful to the officer wives club ladies for catering the reception for I just couldn't do it alone. Besides Guy wanted me to be with him and visit everyone.

The last of the visitors had left and the ladies were cleaning up. They told us they had it handled and to go home. We were to get with my family in the morning as they wanted to have time alone with us. Guy said there was a nice dining lounge at the O Club so we decided to meet them at the gate and show them the way. Bonnie brought Becky and the baby Ryan so I could get a chance to hold him before she drove back the next day.

We had such a great visit and I just wanted to let momma know I would be coming to visit more now that I was well. She was so happy that Bonnie was going to live with me for she was so worried about her home life. Of course I am very contented now that I have Bonnie going with us to Hawaii and finishing school there. Then having Becky come made me very proud that she wanted me to be a part of their lives too. Donny will come around when he doesn't feel like he is dishonoring his father. It is all in God's timing and we all believe that but are thankful he has given us all a new beginning for our lives. They all love Guy and I am proud of him as he fit right in with the guys and had a ball telling jokes and listening to every word they said.

Guys' mom, dad and Bret took off to visit some friends in San Diego but planned to stop by on their way back up to Oregon. They wanted us to have some private time with my family and I really respect them for that. It would have been great for Bret to stay and get to know his step-sister but with Becky there I knew he would feel left out. I told Guy we would have to do it this summer when he got home.

Bonnie and Becky went to the movies so Guy and I got to babysit Ryan and get to know our little grandson a little better. He was so good and slept most of the time even though he was bounced from lap to lap for the last 3 days. Even Guy and I couldn't wait to have some quiet time to ourselves as Bonnie and I would be going home in a few days.

I woke up and went into the living room and found Bonnie, Becky and baby sleeping on the hide-a-bed. I had fixed Ryan a place putting two sofa chairs together right outside our bedroom door but they had put him in bed with them. I didn't want to wake them so went back to bed and told Guy what I found so he pulled me over and we fell back to sleep cuddling each other.

Saying goodbye to Becky and little Ryan was so very hard to do but I knew that this was just the beginning of our bond again. Becky and I had always had a special friendship as she wore her feelings on her sleeve. She was the child that loved life and people so I knew whereever her life would lead her she would be a great friend and of course mother and wife.

## Chapter 26

## Home At Last

Saying goodbye to Guy as Bonnie and I loaded on the plane was so hard. He wanted us to have this time together and make up some of the time that we had been apart. I loved him for that but it was still hard to leave him.

As Bonnie and I sat together on the plane we talked about getting her acquainted with the area, where she would be going to school and plans for shopping for school clothes. She was beaming as we made plans and praising the Lord for answered prayer in her coming to live with us.

Our flight went fast and as we were walking into the terminal I spotted Heather waving. It would be so great to see her again and have my best friend around and enjoy Bonnie's company too. We were jumping up and down hugging and she had tears saying she missed us and was glad we were finally home. Oh, my, that sounded so great! Home at last! I will miss my man but it will only be a couple of months and he will be with us permanently so I kept reminding myself that as I lay in bed without him by my side.

It was Saturday and I was so surprise when Bonnie jumped in my bed this morning saying, 'let's get up and start the day'. What a change for she was my Saturday 'sleep-in-late' girl. We decided to put on clothes to run the beach and then eat breakfast when we returned. As I was dressing the phone rang and to my delight it was my special 'guy' saying good morning and he had great news for us. He told me the doctor at the hospital in Honolulu had called and said they wanted to interview him and also asked how soon he would be able to come if they appointed him. He knew he had not quite 3 months to go and the doctor told him that would be fine but to let him know as soon as possible when Guy could get back for the interview. I was so excited for Guy but I felt so bad that we left him there alone and we were talking about all the fun we were going to have! I decided not to sound too excited so he wouldn't feel too bad. We hung up and off Bonnie and I went to the beach to run and walk.

We decided when we got back to eat breakfast on the patio and then get our showers to make plans for the coming weeks. As we were eating the phone rang and it was Perry at the hospital. He welcomed us home and then said that Guy had told him to have me come in for some blood work. I knew it had been a few months so figured it was time. I had been getting tired but hoping it was just the planning of the reception and trip home. I told him I would be in Monday morning early and he said that would be fine. I had to reassure Bonnie it was just a check-up since I had been gone so long.

Getting out my notebook and sitting down with Bonnie to make our plans, what we would be doing first. It was so much fun and she didn't want to do it all at once but to take in the area and school first. I wouldn't be able to enroll her until August so we had a couple of months to get her ready for that day. I had her make up a list of what clothes she needed for I know she didn't bring everything but she had sent some boxes she had packed with clothes and personal belongings. That afternoon I decided to start going through some of the clothes that Miss Margery had left. We had both bedrooms full but many of the items were too old for Bonnie. Me, I wouldn't need nice clothes for a long time.

Getting up on Sunday was exciting for me as I wanted to introduce Bonnie to some of the families at church. There were some that were high school age so hoped they would welcome Bonnie and give her some pointers about school. On our way home Bonnie said that the group meets on Sunday evening and she was invited to come. I was so happy! We no sooner got into the house when Guy called to say he was coming home for the July 4th long weekend and meet with the hospital board on Monday before going back. I hollered at Bonnie and told her so we decided we would have a BBQ and invite the Connors. I told her if there was a girl at church she wanted to invite she could.

That evening I talked to Bonnie about the items that I had brought home from the crash and asked her if she wanted to be a part of locating the families. She thought that would be so much fun. I told her we would go down to the bank and get the papers and items from my safety deposit box and look at them again. We decided we would do that after I went to get my blood work done at the hospital in the morning.

Monday morning and it was time to go to the hospital. As we walked in I felt different but remembering my stay and the friends I had made. I was looking forward in seeing them all again. I went directly to the lab so I would get that out of the way. Dr Perry heard I was there so came in as I was finishing up and gave me a hug. He said, 'Heather is one happy woman that you are home so maybe now I will get my moody wife back to normal'. We both laughed and he went back to his office. We walked down to see Donna and she was screaming as she saw us coming. It was so great to be missed for I had missed my friends too. Donna took her break and we went down to get some tea in the cafeteria. I was taken back when she told me that her hubby had gotten orders and they were leaving for a base in Florida in 2 months. We both had tears for I don't know what I would have done without Donna all those months that I was in the hospital. She became a wonderful friend. We knew we would keep in contact but that would be two months away so we had lots to do in that time. Bonnie looked at us and said, 'that is the only thing about the military, but we always find new friends where ever we go'. I tagged to that, 'and they are always life-long friends'. Donna hugged me and said, 'for sure'. Bonnie and I left and went to the bank. When I got there I was told that she could not go in with me. I took a box and put the items in it also putting the sword or dagger in to show Guy and Bonnie. The money I still didn't know what or how to tell him yet. Maybe when he gets home to stay I can tell him then.

As we left the bank I decided to go by her high school just so she would get an idea of where she would be going. She was impressed and said that the girl at church whose name was Carrie said she would take her. I was so happy to hear and know that Bonnie was making friends very easy.

We were just coming back from a walk on the beach and the phone was ringing so hurried to catch it. It was Guy and he said, 'How would you like your husband home for good this week-end?' I was crying and trembling and Bonnie came over as she didn't know what was wrong with me. I screamed he is coming home to stay on Friday. We both danced holding the phone and then I realized Guy was waiting for an answer. When I asked him if he heard us, he was laughing and said, 'I think that was a yes that I can come home'. They told him they had gotten a replacement and he could leave. I asked him if they thought he might volunteer to stay on and he said he didn't offer for he wanted to get home to his family. I started crying and then he said goodnight to us both and when we hung up we jumped around again. That night Bonnie asked if she could sleep with me and we could talk. We looked at the list of crewmen and said tomorrow we will call Guam to see where the crew families lived.

For some reason we could not unwind so put in a video to watch a movie and the next thing I knew it was two am and Bonnie was sound asleep. I figured we could watch it again another time.

Bonnie and I were still on cloud nine when we woke up chattering about getting things ready with Guy coming. Bonnie would work on the food list and I would call our friends. I thought if we furnished the meat and drinks our guests could bring potluck. Bonnie thought that would be fun. In talking to Heather we wanted it to be a surprise for Guy. I had to keep Guy away from the hospital because the flyers would say it was a surprise. I was selfish and wanted Friday night just to be Guy and myself so Heather said Bonnie could stay with them. Since the 4th was on Monday, it would give us the weekend to relax and be a family. Bonnie finished the food list of the meats, condiments and such so we left for the commissary. It was so much fun having her here and the excitement she was showing to do this BBQ party. All of a sudden she jumped up and said, 'why don't we make it your wedding reception with just your friends at the same time?' I thought that was a brilliant idea so called Heather and she said she would get on it and make up a flyer to take to the hospital. I told her it would just be those folks for our house wouldn't hold every one of our friends.

On the way to the commissary we stopped at the hospital to use Guy's office to type the list of the guys who were on the plane with me. I knew Guy would help and I really wanted to get this done to return some of the things I had kept. I remember when we were talking to the General he even mentioned he would make some calls if I needed him to help. I knew we would get them all contacted and needed to get it done since Guy was coming home and getting Bonnie ready for school. As I was coming out of Guy's office Perry saw me and motioned for me to come into his office. I thought he was going to talk to me about the BBQ but instead he mentioned the blood work I just had done. He hadn't called Guy and knew he was coming in on Friday so was leaving the decision to him. I asked him what was up and he asked me how I had been feeling. That panicked me and he saw the concern so he quickly added nothing serious. You are still anemic and he was sure I would need another blood transfusion. We will wait until Guy looks at the results. I can't let this bother me with all the things I have to do so another couple of days won't hurt to not tell Bonnie.

I can't believe it is Friday, I said to myself, as I was getting out of bed. I would be taking Bonnie over to Heather's on the way to get Guy. Bonnie had made a sign so after we took our run on the beach she hung it on the patio window so he would see it as he came in the front door. It was pretty windy today so we didn't run very far. We came back to showers and breakfast. Getting out of the shower the phone rang and it was my man!!! He was boarding the plane so I knew he would be here in about 5 hours. Everything was cleaned up and ready but I didn't want any signs to get him suspicious of anything.

Thank goodness we had another fridge in the garage that I could hide the meat in and all the trimmings that Bonnie had helped get ready. The patio tables and chairs were all cleaned so with everyone bringing their own lawn chairs. This would make it so much easier to not bring inside chairs outside. The weather forecast says it is to be a glorious day with only a breeze. How awesome the Lord is for he knows it is a special day for us.

I hollered at Bonnie to hurry up and get ready for we had only one hour and I had to drop her off yet. She came out carrying her small overnight bag and we were off. She said Heather and Perry were taking her to the movies so she was looking forward to that. Heather said she and Bonnie would work on the BBQ and Reception.

Quickly hugging Bonnie as she got out of the car, we saw Heather running out and she stated Perry drop Bonnie over tomorrow evening. I said thank you and off I went.

While I was waiting for Guy's plane to land I had brought my list of crew names and was looking them over when I heard a name over the loud speaker. Was I hearing things or was it the same name on my list. I looked up and saw a woman and two children walking toward the desk and watched them. When they started my way, I jumped up and asked her if her husband was on the plane that went down about four years ago out of Guam. She looked at me and I went on to tell her who I was and she dropped her purse and hugged me sobbing on my shoulder. I led her to a chair and she was grabbing her children saying she was glad I made it and sorry for the long stay on the island. I then showed her my list and pointed to her husband's name and what I had of his. She started crying again but then she told her children it was a happy cry. I asked her to write her new address down and I would send her what I had. I asked her if she recognized any of the other names but she said she didn't because her husband had taken the tour as a one year remote. Just then someone called my name and I looked up to see my handsome doctor walking toward me. As soon as I told him what I was doing he smiled and hugged me. As we walked to the car I told him I would make it up to him for not greeting him the way I had wanted to. He put his arm around my waist and said, 'you just did'. 'How I love this man'!!

As soon as we got home he changed his clothes and wanted to take a walk on the beach. I knew he missed this so we took our time talking and walking. Watching the sunset as we sat on the steps we didn't say a word and when I looked up at him he had tears in his eyes. I asked him if there was anything wrong and he just grabbed me, picked me up and carried me into the house. He said, 'this is what I have missed, you'.

As I was putting dishes in the sink, I saw Bonnie walk in with the Connors. Guy was up and Bonnie was in his arms. Big tears came to my eyes with pride as I listened to them greeting each other. Then Perry and Heather gave him hugs welcoming him home. Heather and Bonnie walked out to me and showed me the plans. They were great and I was so proud of them both for just taking the lead and helping with our July 4th Reception and BBQ. This was a side I had not got the privilege of seeing in Bonnie for her older sisters were always the party planners and now she had come alive to be herself. What joy I am going to have while she is here finishing her schooling. I didn't even want to dream that she might stay on and go to state college. Too soon to ask but not too soon to be praying for the Lord's Will for her life. I just wished I had been there for the other two to share in their future plans. School I could see but getting married is the hardest to overcome and to have a baby grandson seems so unbelievable yet wonderful.

Perry and Guy, as usual, went outside to talk and I had thoughts it might be about my blood work. Not knowing Perry was seeing if Guy wanted to play golf early Monday morning. It gave the three of us women a chance to talk about Monday since Guy would be around Bonnie and me most of the day tomorrow. Bonnie said she would call Heather for she knew I couldn't call unless Guy was in the shower or on the beach. Heather then told me that Perry was coming and taking Guy golfing to get him away from the house. They both said it was going great and thought using that day as our reception would throw Guy off if he found all the food in the garage fridge. Perry and Heather left and Bonnie said she was heading for bed. Guy looked at me with a grin and said, 'that sounded like a great idea'.

I woke up and Guy was in the shower so I went out to put water on and fix breakfast. I went back to wake Bonnie and told her to get her shower and come on out to eat. I love the way Guy appreciates being home for he came out in his robe, remembering Bonnie was in the house now, and started helping me. He put his arms around me just when I was turning the eggs and I had eggs running down the skillet. Taking it from me he proceeded to do another one and was laughing all the time. I told him I missed him in the kitchen and he said, 'by the looks of the stove you must have' and dodged behind the chair. Just then Bonnie came out with wet hair and her robe to breakfast just as we had dished it up. What a beautiful prayer Guy offered to the Lord that morning, now we are home and a family.

After going out to eat after church we all went to change clothes and relax. I wondered where Bonnie was so went back to find her asleep on her bed. I tiptoed out and went to tell Guy she was taking a nap. He then told me he was playing golf with Perry in the morning so wouldn't be fixing breakfast. I told him no problem and we went back to watching the game on the sofa but both feel asleep too.

Monday morning was here and as I was getting dressed I heard the doorbell and figured it was Perry. Just then I heard Guy say that he would get it. I went out and there was Perry winking as I said, 'play well'! As they went out of the driveway I started getting the dishes down out of the cabinet and looked at the list of what needed to be done this morning. I decided I had better eat some breakfast for I would be too busy later and didn't want to get all tired before anyone came. I am sure once this is over I will be going in to have another transfusion. I can't think about that now for today is going to be special for both of us. Pulling out the decorations from the guest room I arranged them in the area of the rooms that I knew Bonnie had planned. I looked at her clip board and decided I would wait until she came out and went to our bedroom to clean it up for guests to use if needed. Heather had put on the flyers for everyone to be here at 2 o'clock. I had planned it where

Guy would come home and hit the shower for he did know of the BBQ so if people started coming he would think that is all we were doing. Then we could get the rest of the signs out for the Reception and all would come together like we planned.

## Chapter 27

## Reception and 4th of July Celebration

I put more water on for tea and I heard a 'good morning' coming in the kitchen. We looked at each other and hugged with laughter telling each other we are now in the 'count-down' stages! Bonnie ate and I drank some tea just as the door bell rang. Looking out the window I saw it was Heather. Greeting her, she is always so cheerful, but she had her hands full. I helped her but knew we needed to get to work.

As we worked together getting the house decorated. Our grill was cleaned and brought to the patio. We had the dishes arranged on the counters with beverage containers and glasses ready to be filled when people started giving their preferences. Bonnie checked things off as they were put in place. I had to rearrange the fridge in the garage to make room for the reception cake. Bonnie had placed the July 4th banners around but left room to add the Reception signs under them when Guy went to get his shower. Even Heather brought clothes for Perry just to make Guy think they both needed that.

Our guests started coming and we placed the food in the fridge. Even General Bradley was able to come and bring his wife and two teen sons. Of course they zeroed in on my Bonnie. I figured I would lose her help but was so pleased she didn't desert her post! Donna joined along with Nancy in keeping the food organized. Everyone loved the patio so they took their chairs out and then some went down to the beach. It was all falling into place and I don't know who was getting more excited to have the guys' home, Bonnie or me! Bonnie had gone in and changed so I decided I would before they got here. I put on some caprice and a blouse that I knew I could remove and put on my long shift when the gals brought out the cake. Bonnie had picked out the music so it was playing softly throughout the house and on the patio. She found 'our' song, *At Last*, so wanted to play it while we were cutting the cake. I was so excited for her as she took over with Heather on her heels. I don't know what I would have done without their help and stopped to go tell them so.

It was close to time when the guys should be coming for I was getting so nervous. They would need a place to park so I put my car in the drive and was going to pull it in the garage when I saw them pulling up. I had left the garage door open and told Bonnie the keys were in the car and if she saw them drive up I would run it into the garage. Heather had told Perry the plan so hoped he would remember. I went out and asked Todd if he would light the coals in both BBQs for I had him bring his from home too. I then took the assortment of meat in the kitchen to get it room temperature while the marinate was working. The tables were full of food and all was ready. As I went out to see how Todd, was doing I heard Bonnie call out that they were here as she ran out to pull the car in. We all tried to act normal and not rush Guy too much. He was so excited to see everyone and came over to kiss me. I said, 'oh my, I think you need to take a quick shower so we will put the meat on'. Perry knew that was his cue to go change his too. The three of us with Todd's help hung the rest of the signs but didn't want to take the cake out until after we ate.

Guy and Perry both arrived on the scene at the same time. Todd told everyone that the meat was ready for people who liked theirs rare. Guy asked everyone to make a big circle out on the patio to offer thanks. It was the most beautiful sight for I had tears when I looked around at all our very dear friends who came to celebrate our marriage and July 4th!

I couldn't believe how much food disappeared but so proud of the ladies for the abundance and no one would leave hungry. We had told the group before Guy came that we would be doing the reception cake after we got things cleaned up and they relaxed for a spell. Some went to the beach and others sat around just visiting.

When we realized people wanted to leave Perry quickly went to the beach to get everyone to come back. As I saw Guy walking up the steps I told Heather to get the cake and I had Todd take the table out. Quickly Bonnie put the cloth on and settings. Guy looked at me and said, 'oh boy, dessert time'. Cameras were brought out and everyone made a horseshoe around the table. I went to the other side and took my finger to motion for Guy to come over. Bonnie pointed to the signs and to the cake. Guy looked at me with this adorable smile that told me he was totally surprised. She quickly turned on the music, *At Last*, and Guy turned to me and danced me around in a circle. It was tight in the corner of the patio. We put the knife in our hands and proceeded to cut the cake when Guy turned to me and said, 'one cut for my beautiful wife God gave me'. We cut one cut and then I replied, 'one cut for the wonderful man God gave me'. Then finished the cut, put it on a saucer and fed a piece to each other very gently. I kissed him with frosting on his lips and then he fed me and kissed me. He didn't stop until he had licked my whole mouth. Everyone was hooting and hollering saying, 'we love you'. I couldn't help but have tears in my eyes and we both said together, 'we love you all too'. What a beautiful day we had as we said our thanks and goodbyes.

I was so proud of Heather, Bonnie, Todd and the girls for all their help in cleaning up for when everyone left the kitchen didn't even look like we had a party! I went in to put a pot of water on for tea for I wanted to relax for the rest of the evening with my family. As I was doing this Guy was calling for 'his girls' to come to the living room. We went in and he pointed to Bonnie to sit on the right and me on the left. He put his arms around our shoulders and told us he had news to tell us. We both looked at him at the same time and said 'What'. He then told us that he had gotten word that he was accepted to come on staff at the Honolulu hospital as soon as his three months were done at Hickam. It was so funny to see the two of us hug him at the same time. He just laughed and said, 'Wow'! I said to him, 'didn't you notice you are loved very much'? He leaned over and kissed Bonnie on the cheek telling her thank you for today and for being here. Then he told Bonnie to please put on our song as he pulled me to the floor to dance. Bonnie yelled as she went down the hallway that she was taking a shower! We just kept on dancing. Later that night he asked me if I could keep a secret and of course I told him I could. He told me that Perry was going to be made the commander of the hospital along with promotion to Lieutenant Colonel. He said promotions were coming out next month so they wouldn't be telling him until then. I was so excited for that meant the Connors would be there for at least another four years. I started crying, kissing him and . . . . oh, yes it had been a great day.

Time had caught up with me and I found it was time to report to the hospital for another blood transfusion. While lying in the bed I was going over the list of families that I needed to look up. I had called General Bradley and he was coming over to help me. Guy was back at work and going over all the things that Perry had done to catch him up on what had happened. I couldn't even tell Bonnie the secret but know she will be just as happy for the Connors.

Guy walked in to check my arm and General Bradley walked in. He laughed and looked at me and then to Guy, then saying, 'Does he not trust the staff anymore with you'? We smiled and I rose up to give him a hug and surprisingly he hugged Guy too. He said to Guy that he had heard about his good news and was happy to hear he wanted to stick with his passion and research that he had studied. Thanking him, Guy asks him if he was coming to help Lucinda with the families of the crew members. He walked over to the phone and pulled it over to the bed table and took my folder telling Guy he was indeed here to do just that.

As I listened to General Bradley on the phone talking to the National Personnel Records Center it was so great to hear his voice in stating why and winking at me while talking. I could not have done that without using his rank. When the Center heard why, they were so very helpful. In fact the general said, 'they are putting someone on this just for you'. I had water forming in my eyes and he patted my hand. It took us through the lunch hour and Donna had come in to remove the IV and gave me food. I told them I couldn't leave until Guy came to take me home. General Bradley said he would take me if I wanted to go early but I told him Donna wasn't going to release me until Guy came for me. The Center was to get back with the general and he said he would call me when he got all the addresses. I told him Bonnie had helped me pack everything in separate boxes so ready to mail.

Bonnie came in saying she was done with her volunteer job of taking magazines around to the patients and thought she would like to do that again. I told her maybe she could be a Candy Striper but not sure which hospital would be best. Maybe that would be something she could encourage the girls at church to get involved in and then we could do a rotation with parents in picking them all up. Guy walked in so he was ready to take his family home.

That night I decided to tell Guy and Bonnie of my find on the island for I really wanted to investigate its origin. Bonnie could even do it as a school project maybe.

I went to the kitchen to pull out some cold grilled chicken breasts and Guy came out to see if he could help. I said, 'how about a salad with grilled chicken'. That pleased him so he was getting out the fixings when Bonnie came in and offered to set the table. I was beaming with so much happiness and started singing, 'We Are Family . . . .' and then they started singing along. While we sat at the table eating I told Guy and Bonnie that while I was on the island I had found a treasure piece hidden in the sand. I told them how I had spotted it walking but had a tough time finding the sparkle again. It took the hurricane type waves to wash the sand away from the cliff wall. I went to the bedroom and took it out of my drawer and carried it out to the table, handing it to Guy first to look at. This is what I found. The boat was coming again, so I couldn't dig anymore to see if there was anything else in the ground. Guy didn't say a word for a bit but kept turning it over and over and looking at the stones very carefully. Bonnie had stood up leaning over his shoulder and kept gasping about it being so beautiful. Then Guy turned to me and asked me, 'You never said a word about this all this time'. I wasn't sure if he was upset with me by his tone but just agreed with him. I said that I wanted to go back and maybe take a small shovel and look for more but the news from the pilots made my mind up that it would be almost impossible. Going on to say that I just didn't know when or how to tell you since you were coming and going and every time I thought I would tell you they had you leave. He told me he understood and asked me what I was going to do with it now. Thinking about it, I told them that I might take it to a museum first. If I took a picture of it to show them they might be able to tell me what is was and possibly who it belonged to. Guy commented that it was a good idea not to take it with me but to take a picture of it and put it back in the deposit box. Bonnie spoke up and said they were beginning to get computers in the libraries and some schools so maybe we could research it too. I put it back in my drawer and when I came out they were eating and very quiet. I asked if they were upset with me for keeping it quiet for so long but mainly addressing that question to Guy. He reassured me that he was not and I told him truthfully that with so much going on, I had really forgotten about it. I knew it was a shock, for it was for me, when I found it, I told them. Guy looked at me and laughed about now he changed his mind about wanting to go to the island. Then said that was a joke!

We all three went to the living room and turned on the news to watch before going to bed. Bonnie came over and kissed me for she was going on to bed. Leaning down to Guy she kissed his cheek and said goodnight. I thanked her again for working at the hospital and she said it was fun and really liked our friends. Guy looked at me and turned the TV off and took my hand and off to bed we went also.

# Chapter 28

# How Many Families Can We Find?

Waving to Guy as he backed out of the garage on his way to the hospital I felt so much peace and contentment. We were now going to be together every day and having Bonnie there to make us a family made me so grateful to God that I went into the quietness of my bedroom and got down on my knees thanking him for these wonderful blessings that I now have in my life. I loved reading the Psalms when I was down. When I was so full of thankfulness, I just sat there feeling so much peace and love from my Father in heaven.

Bonnie's sweet voice broke into my quietness so told her to come and sit with me on the floor. I told her how I felt this morning and she just smiled and said, 'That is what I have been doing in my room'. We hugged with tears and pulling each other up I told her I was so proud that she felt this way. We agreed to get our shorts on and run on the beach before eating and planning the day.

When we got back there was a message from the general that he had a couple of addresses for us so I called him right away. He told me I was to call the one wife and the other was a mother. Thanking him I told him I would do that this morning.

Bonnie and I ate breakfast, showered and then made labels for the two packages we were sending. We carefully packaged up the cookies that we had made so they would not get crushed for the children. I had written a note telling them how much I appreciated the items that I used and what I had used them for. Sealing them up we both went to the post office right away. While out I would take the dagger/sword back to the bank.

After we ran our errands Bonnie suggested that we go by the library and see if they had put any computers in yet. Much to our surprise they had one.

It was early enough that no one was on it. While we searched and searched the best idea we saw that what we have is a dagger. Possibly a Barbarian type with a gold handle with stones embedded in it. Couldn't find a date so will have to try and find more information from a reliable source. So we left and decided to look around the area and found a couple of shopping malls that we could go to but get an early start some morning. Guy told me he would be eating with the staff at the hospital. I knew he was excited to be back and see some who had not come to the BBQ. Bonnie forgot her list of things she needed as far as clothes but we needed to buy a few things from a department store and head for home. I wanted to call the two families anyway and that made it easier than having several all at one time.

I fixed a sandwich for the two of us and then Bonnie went to her room so I called the mother first. As soon as I told her who I was she started crying. I told her I had mailed her sons' things this morning and explained the note in the box. When I told her he was the soldier that pushed me in the raft she said he never thought of himself in crisis times. I then told her, 'that is what makes a good soldier'. She told me a little more about him and I just listened for I knew I wanted to hear about the man who saved my life and picture him as she talked about him. We hung up and I had to wait for a while before calling the wife of the soldier. I couldn't imagine who it might be but really wanted to know if I had any contact with him.

Picking up the phone to call I thought this is harder than I imagined it would be but I have to do this. Thankful that Bonnie had gone in to lay down made it easier for I didn't want her to hear and see me go through it. There was no answer and looked at my watch and thought maybe she was picking the children up from school so would wait for a little bit before calling again. I lay back on the sofa to wait and fell asleep but when I woke up it was one hour later. So I dialed again and a small child answered. I looked at the paper and thought it was the little boy who was 9 years old and his name was Peter. So I asked if it was, and he said yes, so I then asked if I could speak to your mother. He asked who it was and I told him to tell her it was Lucinda. When he said that, she immediately got on the phone. I heard her tell Peter to go play and then said, 'hello Lucinda, I have been waiting on your call'. She said that she was excited to know I had some things that belonged to her husband and would give them to her boys when she felt they were ready to have them. I told her I had mailed them this morning and she said thank you. She told me she had just remarried in

March but would never forget him because he was the boy's father and he was a wonderful father to them. She told me a little about him but I just couldn't picture him on the plane. I was nervous and told her they were all so very nice making sure I was comfortable and I really didn't talk to anyone. I thanked her for talking with me and prayed the boys would know their father was truly a hero to me.

# Chapter 29

# Miracle on Church Street

I hung up and walked to the kitchen to figure out what I was going to fix for supper when the phone rang. It was Beverly from the church telling me the church caught fire last night and would take a lot of money to rebuild it. She was afraid it might not get rebuilt since it was a small church and couldn't see how the people were going to raise the money. I just could not believe that this was happening and the pastor was talking about adding on to it to make it bigger. I told her if she was calling around, to ask people to pray for wisdom and if it was in God's will to rebuild we would need to get some fund raisers going. I told her Satan knew the church was growing and bringing in young people so we had to stand up against that evil one and prove God's people are stronger. She said she would and I told her to let Guy and I know what we could do to help. She said we might have to meet in one of the school classrooms but I didn't know that the pastor had found out. There would not be church this Sunday.

I called Guy right away and he said we have to get a group together and have a prayer meeting tonight. He said he would call the pastor and if it was fine with me we would meet at our house. I told him we could do it but to call back after he talked to the pastor. About 15 minutes later Guy called and said we were going to meet at 7 o'clock and the pastor would call a group of strong prayer warriors to come over. I went over to tell Bonnie and she was coming out of her room. I said we need to make some cookies and nut bread and asked if she would help me. We quickly got to work in the kitchen baking and I thought I would put some meat out to make stir-fry, which is easy to do and one of Guy's favorite meals.

We had just finished supper and putting dishes in the dish washer when our first church member came. Bonnie said she would be in her room if I needed her when we got ready to have dessert. I had laid out cups for tea and coffee and had it ready to turn on for later.

The prayer meeting went wonderful and I could feel the Holy Spirit really present so I knew He would bless our response to calling for His guidance. I got up and went in to ask Bonnie to come and help so off we went to the kitchen. Beverly had started cutting the nut bread, Bonnie put the cookies on a plate and I started the coffee and tea water. Putting the food on the bar counter I figured they could come and get what they wanted and the coffee and tea on the stove. All were so very concerned and word was that no one knew how the fire started. We all said goodnight as each left and Bonnie helped me clean up. Guy came out and put his arms around Bonnie's shoulder and told her thank you for helping me. Then he came over to me and put his arms around my waist and whispered in my ear that he loved this team! I turned around and repeated out loud what he had said and we each did high-fives together. Bonnie went to her room and so did Guy and I. We had a large bedroom with a love-seat and comfy chair overlooking the beach as this is where Guy loved to put himself when he was thing and looking at the sky, stars and waves. He pulled me to his lap and said, 'God has put us here at this little church to support and encourage them, so if you will pray for me and I will pray for you as to how we can be good stewards in our service to Him'. I kissed that man with a strong and passionate kiss and told him I was so proud of the leadership he showed for his church family but mostly for the compassion he felt for his family. I laid there that night thanking the Lord for now I knew why he had allowed me to find that money on the beach. We would help build his church building with more courage to see more families won to his kingdom than ever before in that church. I knew what I had to do in the morning. I knew Bonnie would be going to the hospital with Guy in the morning to do the morning Candy Striper shift so would call the bank and set up an appointment to speak with him.

Getting out of bed and going to Bonnie's room, I woke her early so she could get her shower done and have breakfast with us before they left. She got up and I went back to the kitchen to put coffee on for Guy and tea for me. Mixing up eggs and putting veggies in it to make omelets. I put them on low and went in to get dressed. Guy was getting out of the shower and ready to shave so he went to sit looking up at him. He looked down and said, 'What's up my love? He knew it must be important for I never bothered him but told him to go ahead and shave while I talked. I started talking about the prayer meeting and after we went to bed I couldn't stop thinking about the money I had at the bank. He looked at me and got down on his knee and said, 'the money you have there is for you to do what you feel God wants you to do with it'. I didn't tell him it was money I found. I went on to say that maybe we could give it to the building fund in Miss Margery's memory. He looked at me and his eyes were tearing up and said, 'How did I deserve such a wonderful compassionate wife'? I answered that he would have done the same thing and then he quickly kissed me and said he would have. So I told him I was going to the bank this morning and have the banker put the money in the church's account. I then left the bathroom to check on the omelets.

Going out the door Guy gave me a kiss and said he loved me. Bonnie hollered and said goodbye. I hollered to them that I loved them too.

I knew the bank didn't open until 9 o'clock so I cleaned up the kitchen, made the bed, cleaned the bath room and got dressed. Wow, it was ten after nine and I was nervous but felt peace of God's hand in it. Calling the bank I told them who I was and asked to make an appointment to see the banker this morning. I was put on hold and a minute later a male voice answered as the vice president and I told him I needed to speak with him privately if he had time. He asked me if I could get there at 10 o'clock and I told him I certainly could. I went into the guest closet and found a bag that belonged to Miss Margaret and thought this would be what I will put the money in when I go for my appointment. I decided I needed to take the 'dagger' back so put it in the bag.

Arriving at the bank I had them let me into the safe deposit room and I put the dagger back in and pulled out all the 'island' money and put it in Miss Margery's bag. I went out to sit and wait, praying as I sat there for the Lord to guide my words of how He wanted the funds to be given. I heard my name and looking up saw a tall gentleman come over and introduced himself as Mr. Andrews, the bank's vice president. He proceeded to tell me he is not always at this location but was happy to be here to help with whatever my needs were. I began telling him of the fire and he remarked that he had heard and felt really sad. I told him it was Miss Margery's church and that she had been a member for over 40 years. Then I told him who I was and I had been her caregiver companion till her 'home going'. I told him Miss Margery had money stuck under her mattress and in a chest in her bedroom but could not understand why at the time. Now I know why. I found this money, I told him. I was careful to not tell him I found it on an island but wanted him to think it was the money I found at Miss Margery's home. I told him I thought there was $250,000 dollars there but wanted him to count it. He looked at me and said, 'do you want to deposit it'? I told him, 'no, I want it put in the churches account as an anonymous donor'. He gasped and sat there looking at me and then his eyes welted up with tears and said, 'bless you my child'. He got up and took the bag out of the room and I called at him and said, 'please don't take it out of this room but could you have someone come in and count it in front of us'? He looked at me and said, 'Certainly'. He brought the bag back and went out of the office, but back right away with two ladies. They pulled up chairs at a table in his office and proceeded to count the bills. It took them about 15 minutes and when they turned around they told Mr. Andrews there was a correct amount of $250,000.00. I grinned to myself for I had counted it several times not believing there was that much there. The ladies left and Mr. Andrews took a deep breath and said, 'I am so glad I was here today to see this miracle'. I told him I wanted a receipt but I wanted it to be in my name just for my records. He understood and as I left the bank I got into the car and cried, 'thank you Lord for your love for this church and its families'. I couldn't contain myself so drove by the high school to see if they had posted room assignments yet and saw Bonnie's name. I would bring her back so I drove to the base and to the waiting arms of my husband. He did not have anyone in his office when I arrived, .... coincidence, .... not with my God, I rushed to his open arms as I was crying and he held me knowing how relieved we were at being in God's will. 'It felt so wonderful', I told him, 'because I could feel Miss Margery in the room'. He said, 'Let's go find Bonnie and see if she wants to have lunch with us'.

We ate lunch and then Bonnie and I drove over to Radford High School, which is outside the base. We could see where she has to go and what supplies she needs and then go to the Base Exchange to see if they were having any sales on clothes or anything that she might need for school. As we got out and walked to the front we heard someone calling Bonnie's name. She turned and found her friend, Carrie, whom she had met at church, coming at her. I was so happy for her and whispered a thank you to the Lord. She was just getting there too so we all went in together. Coming out with our lists and Bonnie with her room assignments, she was chattering about having some classes with her friend. I asked Carrie where you girls buy your clothes and shop. She mentioned a couple and I turned to Bonnie and asked her if she would like Carrie to go with us this week. Carrie said that her mom worked so she would love to go. I then asked her if she walked and if she needed a ride home. She answered that she had walked over and would love a ride. I could hear the girls in the back chattering away about BOYS that go to the school. Bonnie asked her if she had heard about the church and Michelle said she lives near so walked over after the fire. We dropped her off and drove home. I mentioned to Bonnie that if she wanted to invite Carrie over sometime she could. You might even get her to volunteer at the hospital as a Candy Striper with you. Oh, by the way Dr Connors called to see if I wanted to be in charge of the Volunteer Committee and I told him I would love to. Bonnie looked at me and said, 'Way to go mom'.

That night after Bonnie had gone to bed and I looked at Guy and said, 'What do you think about the youth sponsor bringing the high school kids over to our house for their Bible Study? I told him I wanted her to get acquainted with the Christian kids and since she has been active in the one in California maybe she would have lots to contribute. He thought that would be a great idea and if I wanted to call the pastor about it then it was fine with him. As we were sitting there the phone rang and it was the pastor! What timing! Guy answered it saying, 'was your ears ringing pastor, for we were just talking about calling you'? They laughed and then Guy got quiet. All Guy said was 'I will pray about it and talk it over with Lucinda too'. Then he told the pastor I needed to talk with him about something. He handed me the phone and when I asked the pastor what he thought about our idea he was thrilled. He said he would have the youth counselor call me as we didn't have a youth pastor yet. Then he asked if I would consider being on the decorating committee to figure out what all was needed in the worship center, class rooms, foyer, office and restrooms. I told him I would pray about it. He said that is why I felt the Lord wanted me to ask you two to help.

I hung up and snuggled up to Guy who was sitting very quiet but I thought he was watching the news. He saw my glance and turned to tell me the pastor told him that the bank had called. I sat there staring at him and he just kept on watching the TV. I poked him and said, 'go on'. He turned and laughed and said, 'you know the rest of the story'! Only one thing he said that you don't know is that he asked me to run the building committee to help start building a new church for the community but told him I would pray about it.

The news on the television was over and off to bed we went anticipating to see what God had planned for us tomorrow.

## Chapter 30

# Where Did The Time Go?

As I sat in our new pew looking around, seeing how God had blessed all the families in this church, I couldn't help but go back almost three years ago.

Looking at my husband as he was reading the bulletin and remembering the moment he came into my life. Then meeting Miss Margery and what an impact she made with her love and teaching me about the things of God. Glancing over to Bonnie who was chattering with Michelle, now in her senior year and what a blessing she has been to me. Then the pastor spoke breaking my thoughts as he began our Celebration of Life Service for our church families. We sang and then he asked if anyone wanted to give a testimony of how God has blessed them in the last year. I had waited for this day when we could be all together in this building that God has provided for us to worship in. As I listened to several I found myself raising my hand. Guy looked at me and was smiling, then looked down as the pastor called out, 'yes Lucinda'.

I stood up and said, 'It has been a little over two years since God brought me here from a deserted island that I lived on for almost three years. Not understanding why he allowed me to survive all that time I sit here and God has told me why.

He reminded me, *'Why do you think I brought this gifted man to care for you, fall in love with you, heal your disease and bless his ministry at the Research Department at the hospital'?*

*'Why do you think I put Miss Margery in your path so you could care for her needs, to bring your daughter to live with you and then marry the man I picked out for you'.*

I started crying and said, 'God has blessed me to where my cup has overflowed and now down into the saucer. I continued, 'what more could I ask of God and He said, '*Child your saucer has yet to overflow*'.

So I cannot wait to see how God is going to use me to overflowing AGAIN'.

CPSIA information can be obtained at www.ICGtesting.com
Printed in the USA
LVOW121538240413

330752LV00005B/167/P